Breathless

In Love with an Alpha Billionaire

Part 1

by Shani Greene-Dowdell

This is a work of fiction. Names, characters, places, and incidents either are the product of the author's imagination or are used fictitiously, and any resemblance to actual persons, living or dead, business establishments, events, or locales is entirely coincidental.

Dear Reader,

I humbly thank you for reading the Breathless series. It has been my pleasure to venture of into the multicultural romance genre and you best believe I have loved every minute. You can expect more titles like this from me, as long as I have you in my corner turning pages.

Best,
Shani

CHAPTER ONE

DESTINY

What in the Hell?

What is it about Jacob Turner? I wondered, as I sat naked in the center of his circular, king-sized bed in his presidential suite at the Marriott Marquis. I'd left my office to go get a cup of coffee around noon. Coffee. Then, explain to me why hours later a stranger had literally charmed my panties off. If anyone told me I would bump into the heir of Turner Enterprises and be in the billionaire's bed by nightfall, I would have cursed them out for suggesting something like that about a respectable woman such as myself.

Turner Enterprises was the nation's number one commercial construction conglomerate passed down for generations through the Turner family. It had offices all over the United States. Turner Enterprises constructed every substantial piece of business property in the U.S.

I could see how Jacob was such a persuasive man in business and in life. His family groomed him since he was old enough to walk to take the helm of the business. He was powerful and damned sure influential. He had manipulated me into forgetting all my values and coming back to his suite after only a few hours of mentally stimulating conversation.

When I looked around the lavish room with gold trimmings, high back chairs and other regal furnishings, I suddenly felt out of place.

"Jacob, I don't think I should be here," I said, while scooting to the edge of the bed. I scanned the room searching for my clothes.

Jacob pulled me back flush to him, hard. My cool skin collided with his burning hot flesh instantly warming me to my core.

"Stay," he breathed onto my neck. "We don't have to do anything you don't want to do, but please stay the night with me. I could use the company."

I looked into his hazel green eyes of privilege. He was used to getting what he wanted, and he wanted me…to stay with him. Jacob could have any woman he desired. Why me?

Questions floated through my mind but dared to leave my lips. I crossed my arms over my bare chest to cover my breasts.

"Okay, I'll stay a little while longer, but only under one condition."

"Anything."

"I need to put on my clothes."

It was my ex-husband, Montie's, weekend to have

visitation with our children, so I really had nowhere to go. I just didn't want to sit naked with a man I hardly knew.

Jacob slid over to the edge of the bed so that he was sitting closer to me. Turning my face to his, he placed a soft, lingering kiss on my lips. His breath absorbing into mine and becoming a part of me made me forget that I wanted to put on my clothes. Instead, I had the urge to straddle his lap and swallow him completely inside my being.

While running my rogue fingers over his smooth, tanned back, I struggled to maintain control of my actions. A deep sigh escaped my lips as I pulled away from him and looked away, breaking our intense stare. I was uncomfortable with how fast we were moving, and he sensed it.

Jacob stood up, went to the closet, and returned with a robe. "Put this on."

His protruding erection spoke his salacious desires loud and clear. But he respected my wishes enough not to press the issue, at least not at the moment. He sat on the sofa on the other side of the room and turned on the television.

"What do you like to watch on TV?" he asked, while scrolling through the many channels available.

"I don't really watch much TV," I admitted, my eyes never leaving his ruggedly handsome face, covered with a curly dark brown beard.

"What is it about you, Destiny?" he asked as he watched me watch him.

"What do you mean, what is it about me?"

He bit down on his bottom lip. "I mean, what is it about you that has me so thrown off. I've never had a woman in my hotel room, unless it was for... you know. But with you, I'm satisfied with just watching you sit there."

"You will have to tell me what it is. You're the one who invited me to your room, Jacob."

"I invited you here, because I know what I want when I see it. And, I didn't want our conversation to end at the coffee shop. I wanted to see more of you...needed to see more of you." His eyes raked over my body showing a strong need that I wasn't sure he would be able to contain much longer.

I needed to get the hell out of there before I did something I would regret. Let's face it; I didn't have what it took to screw a stranger. How I made it this far into this encounter was mind boggling to me. I stood up, put on the robe, and stood beside the bed.

"Well, you've seen all of me. Are you happy?" I joked, as I tightened the robe around my waist.

"I'm the happiest man alive."

"Yeah, right," I mumbled. He really thought he was fooling me with the whole 'act like she's the shit' game he was playing. "I'm sure you say that to all your ladies," I added.

8

"Come sit beside me," he said, patting the spot beside him. It wasn't a request, but an order.

"No, I'm fine right here, thanks." I finally found my voice and started to use it for the first time since I got to this damn hotel. He was fine and all, but if I wanted any chance at not coming off as another thirsty female, giving it up within twenty-four hours of meeting him wasn't the way to go.

"Don't make me get up and bring you over here."

"You're making me uncomfortable talking to me like that," I said.

"Destiny, I just want to talk to you. It's completely innocent." He threw his hands in the air and the most harmless expression covered his face.

"Uh, huh..." I said and walked slowly over to where he sat. He pulled me down onto the couch and pulled the string to the robe to release my bare flesh for his eyes to partake of, again. "Completely innocent, Jacob, this is not..."

My words drifted away as he ran his fingers over my neck, admiring it as if it were a perfect sculpture. He then ran his fingers through my hair and pulled my face to his. Looking into my eyes, he crushed his lips against mine.

Erotic moans escaped my throat alerting Jacob to my satisfaction. Too much time had passed since I'd been touched this way. The war of sexual frustration within was being won by the flesh that wanted what it

9

wanted from the first moment I saw him at the café.

I gave in to the sexual tension that grew between us. My arms flew around his neck as our tongues danced. Tension mounted to epic proportions. Both of our desolate hearts awaited a long, overdue release.

I hadn't had sex in months, and the way he owned my lips said he hadn't felt real passion in just as long. I wanted Jacob in a bad way, and that insatiable craving of this man unnerved me. Being helpless to the overwhelming sensitivity emerging between my thighs pissed me off and drove me crazy, at the same time. My hands ran freely over his body, leaving no place that I could reach untouched. Once I reached his bulging erection, he pulled my hands together and placed them on my legs. He moved my hands to my own lap.

"Touch your sweet pussy."

Caressing each slowly, I moved my hands over each of my breasts. My right hand cascaded over my stomach, then to my thighs. Then, I propped one leg up on the sofa and inched my hand down to stroke my hottest spot, but he stopped me.

"Stop right there," he growled out and replaced my hand with his much larger one. Two of his thick fingers eased inside of me, going deep enough to bring my full attention back to his intense stare.

The greediest eyes I'd ever seen searched my soul, even as a part of me struggled to come to grips with what in the hell I was doing. What kind of mind control did this eccentric, hairy, green-eyed Caucasian man had over me?

I fell back on the sofa and began to wriggle my booty, thrusting my pelvis toward his ravishing fingers. When he intensified his strokes, I screamed out, "Jacob... oh... that feels good!"

"I want it to feel better than good," he said as he removed his fingers, dropped down onto the carpeted floor, and slid my ass to the edge of the sofa. His face disappeared between my thighs, and he tongue kissed my lower lips, pressing his tongue hard against my clit and moving it back and forth in measured strokes.

Jacob held my legs firmly in place, so I could not move, as a violent orgasm poured into his mouth. I jerked uncontrollably, experiencing some type of outer-body state that had never happened to me.

"You are sweet, Destiny. Give me all of that sweet cum." He moaned his pleasure as he lapped up my nectar, not leaving one drop behind.

He sprang to his feet and removed his boxers, as the last ripples of orgasm went through my body. He was bigger than Montie, which made me think hard about whether I wanted him to thrust his unyielding sword inside of my damn near virginal sex.

Before I could say anything to the affirmative or negative, Jacob pulled me into his embrace and seized my lips. "I want to fuck this sweet pussy so bad," he said, rubbing his finger against my clit.

"I want you, too," I said, taking in his magnificent physique. Strong jawline, broad shoulders, toned abs and thighs. He looked kingly as he stood up and walked to his drawer to get a condom out of his wallet.

As I watched this perfectly sculptured, almond milk colored man walk away, I looked at my darker thighs that had lines of cellulite from when I was heavier, dimples and other imperfections. I sat up on the sofa and pulled the robe tight around my body.

"What are you doing?" he asked as he walked back to me.

"It's cold in here. I just need to stay covered up," I lied while avoiding his gaze.

As he applied his condom, he continued to study me.

"Cold?" he said as he walked over to the temperature gauge and turned on the heat. He came back to me, took me by the hand and walked me to the bed. Standing in front of the bed, he kissed me so sweetly that I moaned recklessly into his throat.

This. Us. He was confusing to me. I could've easily gotten it twisted and thought he actually gave a damn about me, if he kissed me like that one more time. I couldn't resist my blazing attraction to him, and that was dangerous.

I didn't even notice him removing my robe again, until he threw it across the room, as if he never wanted to see it again.

"I want to look at you while I make love to you," he said as he laid me down on the bed.

I scooted to the center of the massive bed and opened my legs wide enough to accept him. He crawled on top of me and pushed my legs back further with his arms.

"Oh!" I screamed when he entered me with precision, ripping my canal open without warning.

"Shit, you're tight," he said, as my body gave way to the pressure of his size. Within seconds, he possessed me with every slow and deliberate stroke. I quivered with every thrust, with what seemed to be a constant orgasm.

"What the hell are you doing to me?" I managed to ask between the jerking and quivering that once again, had, taken over my body.

He sucked a pebbled nipple into his mouth.

I trembled and released the hardest orgasm known to women. My release covered his condom clad dick and spilled over onto the bed. He bucked relentlessly inside of me, as my vaginal muscles contracted and released him uncontrollably.

"Oh, shit you're taking this cum from me. I'm coming right with you, baby! Ugh!" he said and collapsed down on top of me, holding me in place, as he jerked out his release.

"Oh, Jacob," I moaned my pleasures as I watched

this amazing creature's body move in awe. "Stay with me tonight, Destiny."

CHAPTER TWO

DESTINY

Breathless

Earlier that day, before I "fell in bed with Jacob," I walked out of Tazi's Cafe in downtown Atlanta, with a piping hot cup of coffee in my hand. Jacob approached the store walking with a measured stride. My surprised brown eyes zoned in on his soft, hazel green gaze. But that wasn't all that had my attention. It was the gush of fresh air flowing alongside him, captivating me.

"Here, let me get that for you," he said, handing me my briefcase that had, unbeknownst to me, fallen from my hand. His gesture of kindness snapped me out of the stupor I had fallen in to.

Perfect.

I looked like a bumbling idiot in front of a guy who had surely just stepped out of a sexy male catalogue.

"Thank you. I can be so clumsy at times," I told him, scrambling to retrieve my belongings from his outstretched hand.

A handsome smile spread across his broad face, as my hand touched his. "It's not a problem. It's always my pleasure to help a pretty lady."

I smiled. "I'm on my lunch break and was rushing to get back. I'm so sorry," I added, embarrassed.

"No need to apologize. The pleasure truly is all mine," he said as his tongue slid noticeably across his lips. His gaze was piercing as he ran his eyes over my body, inch by inch. Tazi's was a small joint with a house full of regulars, so to see an unfamiliar face, *his* unfamiliar face, was refreshing.

"I haven't seen you here before. Do you work downtown?" I asked.

"I'm from Atlanta, but I live in Florida. I'm only in town for a few days visiting my grandmother at her retirement home. And, she told me that I had to check out Tazi before I left Atlanta, so..." He humped his shoulders. "Here I am. What do you suggest off the menu?" He ran a hand through his silky, dark brown hair, as his eyes fixated on me, awaiting a response.

Suggest? What if I suggested the sexy creature have me for lunch? I could've lain across the counter and let him feast upon me until he was full. My thoughts ran rampant with lust, until I remembered my mantra. Yeah, I was saved and single. Ever since I divorced Montie Brown, I walked the straight and narrow line of avoiding relationships that would lead nowhere but to the bedroom. So far, I did an impeccable job of avoiding fake love.

I took a *deep* breath of his fresh air, because yes, all of the air surrounding me belonged to the man standing before me. I silently meditated for strength to breathe on my own.

"So what do you recommend?" he asked again, to which a throaty voice I didn't recognize belted from my lips.

"Oh, I guess, the three-layer chocolate mousse cake is a winner," I replied with a firm clearing of my throat to rid myself of the imposter in my vocals.

"I'll definitely try the chocolate," he said with a wink.

An awkward moment passed between us, and I felt the need to fill the dead space. "Are you originally from Atlanta?" I asked.

"Nah, my family has roots here, but I was born and raised in Miami."

"Oh, well enjoy your first visit at Tazi's. You're going to love it." I took one last look at the sexy man and stepped around him.

"I didn't get your name," he yelled out as I reached for my car door handle.

"Destiny."

"I'm Jacob."

"Nice to meet you, Jacob."

"So, have you tried the three-layer chocolate mousse cake before?" he asked, as he strolled over to me.

I pulled my treat out of the small box inside my briefcase and said, "Yes, this is a smaller 'to go' version of the cake. I order mine this way, because I can't afford the calories of an entire slice."

His eyes lit up, and I became self-conscious under his glare. I was about to open the door and jump in my car, when he said, "Every calorie looks good on you."

"Thanks."

"Would it be too much for me to ask you to share a chocolate mousse cake with me?"

I looked around at all of the skyscrapers downtown. Somewhere in the distance, my empty home office was waiting for me to get back to a pile of work.

"I wish I could, but I really have to get back to work."

"You look like you could use a break, and I could use the company."

I studied his chiseled, tan face and considered his offer. Something hid behind every word he spoke; something intriguing enough to make me drop my keys back inside my purse and say what the heck. It was a public place. It was just dessert. Just conversation.

"Sure. I'll have dessert with you."

I entered Tazi's with Jacob and soon found out the reason he had me at hello. Our personalities meshed like yin to yin and yang to yang; we had so much in common. We just clicked as we laughed, talked, and ate dessert before ever sharing a meal together.

Before the end of the night, I was entangled in his covers listening to Chris Brown and Jordin Sparks sing their duet, "No Air," on Pandora. I shook my head at the thought of being unable to breathe without a man. It was laughable. Something as essential as air was nonnegotiable for me, until Jacob Turner took my breath away.

After our night together, I had soul searching to do. I had vowed to spend time enjoying the single life with the return of my maiden name, Destiny Baker. I planned to take some much needed time off from the thing so many people called love.

And I was good without love. I had a fulfilling job, beautiful home, dependable car and two charming kids. I was newly divorced, and my ex-husband was an awesome co-parent. With all things considered, I had it all.

But as each day and night passed by, since the day I met Jacob, it was so hard for me to breathe when I wasn't with him.

CHAPTER THREE

JACOB

Standing in the Gap

"That will be all, Henry. I'm going to stay here tonight," I said to my driver as he pulled up in front of Justine's condo. It had been a month since I invited Destiny back to my hotel and made the sweetest love of my life. I missed her. I yearned to see her again, but, as a man in charge of a massive enterprise, many working nights and days flew by at the speed of light.

"Okay sir. I will see you in the morning, unless you call before then," Henry said with a tilt of his hat.

I exited the Bentley and Henry drove off. I walked up to my dear friend's doorstep. Justine called me earlier sounding like she had been in a train wreck. I was in the middle of a meeting and couldn't talk, but, when she said she felt like she wanted to commit suicide, I immediately dropped everything and came to her house.

I could've called her parents or an ambulance, but I knew she would freak out if I didn't show up in person.

Therefore, I cut my meeting short and rushed over to check on her.

I was no fool, though. She probably just wanted me to spend the night. She wanted me to make love to her. She wanted our relationship to be the way it was before I broke things off, when I realized that I loved her, but only as a friend.

In the last month, I attended hundreds of meetings about offices opening in Wyoming and Delaware, which were the only two states Turner Enterprises didn't have a local office. It had been busy time for me with lots of activities going on at Turner, so I didn't have time to talk to Justine. That was probably why she was in meltdown mode.

I preferred to finish my business for the day, but I had to be sure Justine was safe before I dismissed her suicide claim as just another one of her tricks to spend time with me. I didn't know what to expect when she opened the door.

"How are you, Justine?" I asked as I stepped upon the doorstep.

"Better, now that you are here," she said, showing a glimpse of her flawless smile. "Come in."

She turned and walked away. I followed her into the living room that the best fashion designer in Miami crafted for the two of us, when we were a couple. A blend of white and beige colors matched Justine's regal personality. A splash of red and orange in a floral portrait over the fireplace fit her sometimes eccentric behavior perfectly.

"Justine, you called me like you had an emergency. What's going on?" I asked.

She sat down on the sofa and stared off into space.

"Talk to me, Justine!"

"Do you want something to drink?" she gestured toward two wine glasses and a bottle of Henri Jayer sitting on chill in the middle of the coffee table.

My mouth watered for my favorite wine, but I shook my head. "No, thanks. I don't want anything to drink."

She lit a candle in the middle of the coffee table.

"Will you tell me what the matter with you is? You were in tears and saying you wanted to kill yourself when you called me, and that's why I'm here," I got straight to the point.

"You left me alone, Jacob. I can't survive like this," she cried, tears welling up in her sky-blue eyes. "How could you just up and leave after all we shared? If nothing else, we were friends...and you...you," she wept as her words caught in her throat.

I ran my fingers through my hair and sighed.

I sat down beside her on the sofa.

"I didn't just up and leave you, Justine. We started out as friends and we will always be friends."

She sprang from her seat and wagged her finger in my face. "I don't want to be just your friend! How can we just be friends, after what we shared? I gave you all of me and you left me alone!"

I stood up and looked at her anguished face. I loved her dearly and respected our friendship, but I didn't have time to spare on this type of stress. If she had been anyone else, I would have had Henry double back so fast that her head would be spinning.

Justine meant something to me, though. She had been my best friend since kindergarten. She defended me when other kids picked on me, and she added acceptance to my life before I understood dividends and assets.

"Justine, stop crying." I hugged her close. "I'll always be here for you. I love you, girl."

A sparkle of hope gleamed in her eyes. "If you love me, why are you treating me like this?"

She tilted her neck, and I knew she wanted a kiss. I gave it to her—a more than friendly kiss on her lips, then pulled away and kissed her forehead. I thought of the best way to tell her I was falling for another woman.

"I don't want to see you hurt like this. It's just that..."

"What, Jacob?" she asked as her light eyes darkened.

"You know what, it's not important. Go get yourself all dressed up and we're going to go do something fun.

Like back in our college days," I said, unable to bring myself to crush her when she was already so fragile.

"Like old times?" she asked, as she grinded her thin body against mine.

"Justine, go get dressed." I sighed. I hated the feeling that I was giving her false hope. I had to find a way to let her know it was over romantically, and to get my friend back.

"It won't take me that long to get dressed." She shrank away from me and pranced toward her bedroom. "Thanks for spending time with me, Jacob," she turned around and said humbly.

"No problem, Justine. Now, go get dressed."

Giggling, she ran off to her room, leaving me to figure out how we got to this place.

We spent twelve years at St. Mary's Catholic School. We attended sleepovers, family dinners, and parties through elementary and high school. I consoled her, after a creep that was supposed to be her soul mate left her at the altar. I stood in the gap that her fiancé, Rick, left wide open. One thing led to another after I gave her a ride home from the chapel that day. By nightfall, Justine and I melded into one, releasing deep tensions our past lovers left behind.

Soon things were hot and heavy between us. Our parents were happy, and even though our romantic relationship had been a rebound affair, she was safe for me. She had been by my side since kindergarten.

She wasn't just another chick trying to get the Turner name, and that was good enough for me, until Destiny walked into my life, stole my attention, and demanded my affection.

Destiny's beautiful smile lit a fire inside of me. Her sensual moans awakened every part of me. I had been a one woman's man, but something about Destiny made me want more than a safety net. She made me want to walk on the dark side of love, where only my heart guided me. I didn't want a best friend; I wanted burning passion. It would crush me if Justine ended her life because I followed my heart. I didn't want to let a part of me die on the inside, either.

I stared at Justine's closed bedroom door and thought about how I would tell her that it was over for us. I planned to take her to hang out and then come back and sleep on her sofa. It would be a night out amongst friends, something she would have to get used to. Then, I would tell her everything in the morning.

My vibrating cell brought me out of my thoughts.

My heart leapt in my chest as I answered.

CHAPTER FOUR

DESTINY

Crave

I walked with a high stride, when I stepped off flight 1087 in Miami, Florida. I claimed my bags from baggage claim, retrieved my rental car from Avis, and was on the highway headed to my hotel within thirty minutes. Just knowing I was in the same city as Jacob made me all giddy. I dialed his number.

"Hello," he answered on the third ring.

"Hey babe. Are you busy?"

"Not too busy for you. What's up?" he asked.

"I bet you can't guess where I am. I just bet you can't," I beamed, as the big ole country grin on my face caused a driver passing by to smile, as well.

"In Miami?" he asked with not quite as much enthusiasm as I would have expected. Given our heated phone call the night before, I thought he would be turning corners already, since we had a chance to see each other in the flesh.

"Yeah..." I answered slowly, gauging his response, "I'm meeting a Miami client tomorrow, so I thought I would surprise you."

"You thought you would surprise me?" he said as more of a question.

"Yeah, but if you're busy this weekend, I definitely understand."

"You are just full of surprises, aren't you, Ms. Destiny?"

"I try to keep things popping," I said with a laugh.

"You definitely do that. Who do you have a meeting with?" he asked.

"Susie Alexander from Museum of Contemporary Art? I'm hoping to start doing some marketing for them."

"Oh, yeah. Susie is a good person. Do you want me to call and put in a word?"

"No thanks, sweetheart. You've done enough by introducing us. I can handle her on my own from here," I said, thankful for his willingness to help. "But... I do want you to come and put in a good night's work with me," I teased, smiling from ear to ear.

"Destiny..." he began to speak, but I was so excited I continued to talk.

"You can meet me at the Embassy Suites at the Airport. It's not a presidential suite or anything like that, but I really want to see you."

There was a long pause on the line, as if he was thinking about whether he wanted to spend the night with me.

"That's okay, if tonight is not a good time for you."

"Yeah, it's bad timing. I have a lot going on," he finally admitted in a dry tone.

"I need to get rested up tonight, anyway," I said, and it took everything in me to not sound disappointed.

"How about I take you to lunch after you meet with Susie tomorrow?"

"Lunch will be fine," I said as the wind deflated from my chest. A long, drawn out pause loomed over the line.

"Sorry Destiny."

An apology wasn't enough to ease the unexplainable feeling of rejection that came over me. He had nicked my ego, but I would be fine. I steered into the hotel's parking lot and found a parking space. "No, it's okay, Jacob. Tomorrow is fine. I'll see you then."

After late night texting, X-rated phone calls, and fantasizing about what we would do if we were in each other's arms again, we were only a few miles away and he had something more important to do. I tried to understand that he was the brains and brawn for his family's beloved company. But, he had hundreds of employees at his disposal. He should be able to get any of his qualified workers to free him up for one night. I couldn't think of one logical reason why he couldn't make time for me.

"I'll be there as soon as you get out of your meeting tomorrow, Destiny," he promised.

"Sure, you will."

"Destiny?"

"Yes," I said, ready to hang up the phone, take a hot shower, and sink into the comfort of my hotel bed. At least, the bed would be there to hold me tight, all night.

"I'll make this up to you," he said with his voice low, as if he were whispering his words directly to my heart. "I hope you understand."

"I understand," I told him, and part of me did understand. He couldn't stop his life just because I popped into town – never mind that I arranged a business meeting almost eight hundred miles away from home two weeks before Christmas, just to see him. I was used to men putting work ahead of me. My ex-husband Montie did it for years.

Me being in Miami was obviously nothing extraordinary. Jacob was a powerful executive, with many willing women at his disposal. Hell, we'd had sex on our first night.

After taking a deep gulp to swallow the growing lump in my throat, I disconnected the call, threw my cell phone into my purse, and attempted to remove the huge dagger that hung from my chest.

CHAPTER FIVE

DESTINY

I'm in Love

Instead of sitting around sulking, I called my cousin, Tasha, who lived on the upper east side of Miami. She had been asking me to come to Miami so we could hang out. Maybe she could show me a little bit of the city where the magic happens, since my plans to be with Jacob were a bust.

"Hey Tasha," I feigned excitement when she answered on the first ring. It wasn't that I wasn't happy to talk to her; I was just let down by Jacob.

"Hey girlie!" Tasha beamed through the phone. I could hear the love and surprise in her voice, at once. "To what do I owe the pleasure of speaking to my favorite cousin this evening?"

"Well, earlier when I was breezing through the streets of Miami, headed toward the Embassy Suites, I thought I'd give my bestie cousin a call and see what we could get into."

"You've got to be kidding me right now! Who, what, when, where, and how did you end up in Miami?"

I laughed at her silly butt. "You're still a mess. I'm sorry I didn't tell you I was coming to town, but I'm most definitely here. I have a meeting tomorrow, but I'm free to have a good time tonight."

If things had gone my way, I had no intentions of coming up for air the entire weekend, much less hanging out with Tasha. Yet as I talked to her, I couldn't imagine coming to her city and not hanging out with my cousin.

"So...you came *all* the way to Florida, and conveniently forgot to tell me you were coming? What's really going on?" she asked with a playful attitude.

"I have some business to handle with MOCA, and that's why I'm here. In the meantime, we can get together and have a few drinks."

"Did you say drinks? I can definitely use a drink, after the week I've had," she said.

"Can you meet me at the Embassy Suites by the airport at six?"

"Embassy Suites at six. Yes, ma'am. You already know I'm there. They have that free happy hour, too... I am so there. Where are my shoes?" I heard her snap her fingers for emphasis.

I imagined Tasha frantically searching for her shoes and shook my head. My kinfolks were something else.

"Ha. See you then, girl. Love you," I said.

"Love you too, sis," she replied before disconnecting the call.

I entered the hotel and checked into my room. The first thing I did was go to the bathroom, freshen up, and put on something comfortable.

As soon as Tasha arrived at six, we headed down to the bar area. I was so happy to see her, but I had to force a smile when I thought about the fact that it should have been Jacob with me. Once Tasha and I had our first round of drinks in hand, we found a table to sit and relax for a while. It was then that she gave me a suspicious once-over.

"So, are you going to tell me about this guy, or what?" She shot me a "and don't lie" look.

"What are you talking about?" I almost choked on my drink.

"I'm talking about this guy that has my cousin a thousand miles from home on a Friday night, acting uptight and, if I could call it, a bit sad at the moment."

"What do you mean, Tasha?"

"Look, I know that you love me. I also know you didn't travel into town a day early for a Saturday meeting, just to surprise me with free drinks at your hotel. You're a planner and you're cheap. You would have called me to stay at my house, unless you had other plans."

"You think you know me, huh?"

"Like a book. You plan your business so that every minute is accounted. If you wanted to hang with me tonight, we would have had a game plan. You might as well go ahead and spill your guts. You sounded a bit pathetic when you called me, too." Tasha tilted her wine glass toward me and continued. "Go ahead and give it up. Give up the who, what, when, where, and how about this gentleman. If my gut feelings are correct, you may need a coochie intervention."

"A coochie intervention? You know what; I'm not even going to chase that one." I ran my fingers around the rim of my glass, while deciding what I wanted to share with Tasha. I could have lied and said there was no man involved, but what was the use? We grew up in the same house, like sisters. Tasha knew when my emotions were all over the place, even though I was trying to hold it together.

I remembered when I was a little girl and I took my first five-finger discount. It was a bag of chips from Red and White's grocery store. She looked at me with crumbs all over my face and said, *"You didn't have no money for that."*

I finished off the chips and threw the bag in the trash.

"Yes, I did! Grandma gave it to me," I answered, before swiping my tiny hand across my lips to wipe away the crumbs.

"Who, what, when, where, and how did Grandma give you money and not give me any? I'm gonna go ask her. And you better not be stealing." Tasha stomped back to Grandma's house, just as aware then, as she was sitting across from me at the bar, of what was going on with me. Whenever I was messing up, she would say who, what, when, where and how. I hated that her second-grade teacher taught her the five "Ws."

"Well..." I looked around the serene dining area. I had to give her answers, but how could I admit my situation? My heart swelled, and a tear threatened to roll down my cheek. "I think I'm in love."

CHAPTER SIX

DESTINY

Opposing Magnets

After telling Tasha how Jacob made me feel alive, I told her about his family business, the fact that he was a very affluent white man, how we met and continued to communicate for the past month. In Tasha, I had an outlet. She didn't judge me. Eventually, she would give me her honest thoughts and keep it real, but she simply listened.

"Is he at least fine?" she asked, and my eyes glazed over thinking about how sexy Jacob was.

I felt remnants of his touch all over my body as I remembered every inch of him. I was never the type to fall so hard, so fast. It was unusual for me to be in love with a man I had only known a month.

"Yes Lawd, he is so fine. He makes this sister speak in tongues."

Tasha shook her head. She knew I was gone. "Girl, I think you're going to need more than that coochie intervention. We may have to do an exorcism to get Jacob out of your system."

"Whatever." I waved at her. "It's not like that."

37

"Destiny, you should have told me about him as soon as you met him. I could have been checking him out to make sure he's on the up and up. Now, you're all in your feelings and it may be too late."

"I didn't want to start a new relationship playing games. I want to be able to trust my man."

"That's all fine and well, but the truth shall set you free from all binds. Just like tonight, you have no clue as to what he is doing or who he is doing it with, while you are sitting here with your cousin that you've been neglecting for years."

"You're right," I admitted. "On both issues."

"I know you'll always love me," Tasha gushed. "I just don't want you to get caught up with this rich guy," she added in a serious tone.

"I don't want to get caught up either. I have so much going for myself right now. Being drawn back into a relationship where I'm doing the most is the last thing I need. And, being head over heels for a man that puts work, and whatever else, before me and my kids is like going back to Montie."

"Yes, and you know how that story ends. You need to stay grounded. The last time we talked, you said you rededicated yourself to church. Use your faith to keep you on the right track."

"Yeah." I sat frozen.

I wished I could say my infatuation with Jacob hadn't altered my newfound spiritual walk. I wanted to say my faith kept me pure. Aside from the one sin of reliving my fantasy of falling into Jacob's bed at the drop of a hat, I had been walking the straight and narrow.

I wanted to say many things that I couldn't, because they simply were not true. I spent the past four Sunday mornings lying in bed, seduced by Jacob's voice. He'd offered to fly me to Florida on his private jet, but I managed to keep the distance between us, afraid of falling deeper in love with him.

Tasha tapped her fingers on the table. With a half-smile, she said, "Okay Destiny, you need to get all of this off your mind for a while. Let's go dancing. Then tomorrow, when we're not sipping on the devil's water, we'll have a heart to heart about if Jacob is healthy for you."

"That sounds good, except I'll pass on dancing." I shook my head. I loved to dance around in private, but I could not dance a lick.

"Come on, Destiny. Let your hair down and let's have some fun."

"What are you trying to prove by getting me on the dance floor, anyway? Don't you think my pride has been damaged enough for one day?" I laughed and she joined in with my laughter.

The hotel's deejay, who had been playing what sounded like elevator music all night, put on Beyoncé's

"Single Ladies", and Tasha began gyrating in her chair, grooving to the beat.

"Oh, honey, it's true you have no rhythm, but that's not what dancing is about. It's about your body becoming a piece of fluid artwork and losing yourself in the music. It doesn't matter how you look doing it, as long as you feel good doing it."

"I don't know about that," I said and took another swig of my drink.

"I promise, if you go out with me, you will feel better in the morning." Tasha flipped her long, straight hair over her slim shoulders. "You can even praise dance, if that will make you feel better about it."

I giggled and tossed back the rest of my drink. "You are too much, Tasha. That would be blasphemy."

"Yeah, but honey, if we can't have fun in this life, what's the use in living it?" she asked.

Looking at her gyrate and groove in her chair made me remember why I loved Tasha so much. She was the most carefree person one could ever meet. She had a way of making people feel like their problems could be talked, drank, danced, or bible-quoted away.

"You do know you are committable to a mental hospital, right?" I told her with a wave of my hand.

As my hand waved in the air, I examined my empty ring finger with mixed emotions. I was no longer Montie's wife. The budding relationship I thought

Jacob and I had now was questionable, at best. I felt single and alone.

"Shoot, after a good dance partner puts his moves on you, you may be committable to a mental hospital, too. It may help you forget all about what's his name?"

"Jacob," I said, imagining the way his handsome face contorted as he eased inside of me the first time. Forever imprinted in my mind was the image of the pleasure in his hazel green eyes. I couldn't shake him if I wanted to. The thought of him had me buzzed in all the right places. "It is Jacob, and honey the way that man flows through my veins, I doubt I will forget him anytime soon."

"Just hopeless," she said, grabbing her purse. "Come on, let's go."

"Okay," I relented. I dropped a tip on the table and we walked to the car. When we got to the car, Tasha stopped by the driver's door without unlocking it.

"What is it?" I wondered what made her stop and stare at me.

"I hope you are keeping in mind that Jacob could be some privileged man that's only looking for a little exotic fling. Those types of men have a different girl every day of the week. They get their fantasies fulfilled by us, and then go and marry a white girl."

"I've thought about that. I don't think Jacob is like that."

"I'm just putting it out there for you to think about."
She popped the lock to the car and got in.

I didn't appreciate her insinuating I was some
exotic fling for Jacob, but what if she was right? I flung
the passenger door open and plopped down on the seat.
I didn't speak a word as we took the drive to Lapidus
Lounge. I didn't know if Tasha took the scenic route,
so I could think, or so we could clear our minds and
sober up, but it was definitely a long ride.

"We're here," Tasha said, as she pulled up to the
lounge. She touched up her makeup in the mirror.

I took out my makeup bag and freshened up my
face, as well. I was a little uncomfortable with the
scenery once we walked in. The mixed crowd was thick
and kind of bourgeois; a little different from the
parties I was used to, where down to earth people
greeted you with a smile.

Ritzy acting chicks looked me up and down, as if I
didn't belong in their atmosphere. Preoccupied men
looked right through me as they laughed and talked
amongst themselves. I'd just as soon be in my suite
going over paperwork for my meeting the next day
than standing around with this bunch of assholes.

Tasha, on the other hand, didn't seem fazed by the
reckless eyeballing by the women. The first tall, dark
and handsome guy to come along and offer her a drink
had swept her away. I watched as she did everything
from the salsa to Mediterranean dances, for the next

thirty minutes. I was just about to go get her to tell her I was ready to go, when I felt a familiar breeze blow right past me. I turned in the direction of the draft and sure enough found the source.

Jacob.

My mouth flew open with surprise.

I didn't know whether to be excited or pissed the hell off that he was in the lounge, and not busy working on some highly important project.

Gravity pulled me toward him. Gliding in his direction, I paid close attention to the company he kept. I didn't want to barge in on his group and have them think I was some mad, black woman, but who could work against gravity?

I definitely couldn't.

I continued toward him with a feeling of mixed emotions. On one hand, I couldn't wait to wrap my arms around him and kiss his greedy lips. On the other, I wanted to tell him a piece of my mind. How could he think hanging out at a club was better than hiding out in my hotel room for the weekend?

My eyes popped open when an impeccably gorgeous woman, with flowing blond hair, slid forward and sat on his lap. She didn't just sit on his lap; she straddled him and draped her thin arms around his neck. If I didn't know any better, I would have thought the woman, who looked like she just stepped out a model catalog, owned him. He held the mini-skirt clad, long-legged beauty in a loving embrace, as she clung to him. Their admiration for each other equally matched. Her milky skin glistened under the dim chandelier hanging over their table. Her long hair flung to one side as she wrapped her arms around his neck and kissed his lips.

He didn't notice I was there, as the woman drank, uninhibited, from his lips. I stood in shock as the reason he wasn't with me was blatantly obvious. I suddenly felt naked standing there in a plain black dress and heels with a natural coat of makeup.

Jacob and I became opposing magnets, as then I felt pushed in the opposite direction. I carefully shrank away, remaining unseen. I rushed to find Tasha. When I found her, I opened my mouth but sound failed me. Words failed me. I could not speak. I just held my mouth open gasping.

"What the fuck is wrong with you?" she asked, concern etched on her face. "You look like you've seen a ghost."

I struggled to breathe. I grabbed her hand and pulled her toward the door, her feet dragging behind her. When we reached outside, I coughed the crisp night's air into my lungs. She was right. I had indeed seen an evil ghost.

"Destiny, what's going on? You're scaring the shit out of me," Tasha asked, placing her hand on my back. "Do I need to call an ambulance for you?"

44

"Ja...Jacob...I just need some air."

"Is he in there?" she asked, but I couldn't reply. "Come on, Destiny. I'm going to take you back to your hotel." She directed me to her car, and we rode in silence.

I watched as the cars passed by, with no one in Miami caring that my love life was spiraling away. That woman clutched Jacob as if he was her next breath. And, I knew what was going on.

Tasha pulled into the parking lot, put the car in park, and rushed around to help me out of the car. I walked around in a daze. I truly felt lost. I casually directed her to my hotel room, barely acknowledging where we were going. She dug in my purse to remove the hotel key and let us in.

I sunk down in the chair the minute I touched the floor in my room. I could tell that she was scared to say a word.

"Destiny..." she began.

I eventually lifted my gaze to meet hers. "Yeah."

"Maybe it wasn't the best idea to go out, but what happened upset you?"

"Jacob...I saw him in the lounge." I closed my eyes as the words tumbled out into reality. "He was with another woman. She was all over him."

Tasha stared at me until she had to turn away from my miserable, teary face. "First of all, you're going to put your chin up and realize that what you saw is for the best," she fussed. "And, I know that's not what you want to hear, but it's what you need to hear."

"You don't get it. I don't know why I thought you would. No one will understand how I feel," I argued.

"You have known him, what…all of five minutes?" I rolled my eyes, but allowed her to continue. "He leads another life, and you were blessed enough to find out early. You should rejoice in that. If you thought you were the only person in his life, then you were naïve. And now you know the truth."

My mind wasn't ready to accept that. I wondered if there was a logical excuse for him to be hanging out with a woman comfortably in his lap, *kissing* him. I cursed myself for even going there for him, when there was no excuse. I didn't care if we had been together only five minutes, I didn't deserve the lies.

"But, I have strong feelings for Jacob. I told you that."

She nodded. "Oh, I know you *did* have strong feelings for him, but now that you know the real him, things change. Isn't it better to see this now?"

Tasha was right. I was relieved to know I hadn't spent years wrapped up in his lies. But, I was far from feeling better. "I don't want to be alone tonight," I confessed, getting up to go sit on the bed. I kicked off my shoes and lay on the bed on top of the covers. "Stay here tonight, Tasha."

Tasha smiled. "I wasn't going anywhere, anyway."

"Thanks bestie," was the last thing I said before remembering the look on Jacob and his lover's faces as they passionately embraced one another. The pain in my heart caused my lids to close and flutter until I slowly drifted off into a sorrowful slumber.

CHAPTER SEVEN

DESTINY

Against All Rationale

I woke up at eight in the morning. I opened my eyes to see Tasha sleeping across from me on the couch. I went into the bathroom to freshen up. I needed to make my ten o'clock appointment and there wasn't much time left.

After stepping out of the shower and getting dressed, I walked into the room. Tasha was up stirring around.

"Good morning," I spoke, brushing out my hair. "Thank you for staying last night."

She smiled, shrugging, "Hush chile. It's no biggie. Do you feel better?"

I hesitated for a moment, and then went back to brushing my hair. "I'm not completely over it, but in time I'll be fine." I spoke the words, hoping I would soon believe them.

"You sure will be fine. Granny didn't make us out of straw. She built some strong, brick house women and we will not let her down."

"You're right about that, Tasha." She had our grandmother's smile, and seeing it made me smile. I stepped into my stockings, and said, "I hate to jet off, but I have this meeting."

Jacob was still going to stop by and see me after the meeting. I didn't know how I felt about that, but I would figure it out once I saw him.

Tasha stretched and popped her muscles in her arms and back, after scrunching on the sofa all night. She walked over to me and pulled me into a hug. "I have a few errands to run today, anyway. I'll call you later," she said.

"Okay." I pulled from the hug and slid on my black pencil skirt. "Talk to you soon."

She left the hotel, and I finished dressing in a ruffled shirt, pulled my hair back into a long ponytail, and put on my glasses. I glanced in the mirror. Minus my weary eyes, I looked professional; I just hoped my best foot would move forward for the meeting.

I hurried out of my room and down the elevator, heading out to my car. Driving to MOCA, my heart beat fast as I thought about what I was going to say to seal the deal. I wasn't usually nervous when it came to meeting potential clients, but this was a big deal. I had to make a good impression. A victory in business would counterbalance what was going on in my personal life.

"Arriving at address 125th Street on the right," the GPS voice said.

I saw the huge building and smiled. I parked and walked inside MOCA with confidence in my stride. Susie was at the door waiting for me, when I arrived on her floor.

"Ms. Baker, I'm glad to finally meet you."

"I really appreciate you taking the time to meet with me on a Saturday. You must be very busy, Ms. Alexander."

"No problem. I've heard good things about your firm. So tell me about all of this good press you plan to use to take MOCA to the next level," she stated, once we were past the pleasantries.

I took a seat in an oversized black leather chair that was in front of her oversized desk. She sat pensively in her boss' chair with a Scarface-intense stare, expecting my response.

"By the time I'm finished recreating your image, you will not recognize your own company on paper, and that's a good thing. I'm going to portray your art museum's already great image as a source of art and literature on an international platform. People who have been here will want to come again just to see what they missed the last time. New visitors will flock to your museum whenever they travel to Florida."

"And how exactly do you propose to do..."

I cut her off expectantly. "First, I have studied your target audience to see what kinds of things they like to read, eat, and watch on TV, all the way down to the types of underwear they purchase."

"Oh..." she said, sounding impressed.

"I intimately know your customers so well that I can tell you who they are by name. Knowing who they are, what they like, and when they like it, I am able to pitch a message to them that says *MOCA* is the missing piece to your life's puzzle. I will show them how consistently supporting MOCA's functions will enhance their lives."

I opened up my laptop, turned on my sales presentation and went over all of the key products I would put into place for her company, including text messaging for museum lovers, calendar mailings, and trade shows. Once the final slide was up, Susie was ready to sign on the dotted line.

"Where do I sign, and when can we get started?" she asked, sounding enthusiastic about a partnership.

"Right on the dotted line and we can get started as soon as Monday," I responded, whipping out my PR contract.

I loved my career. I was such a natural at convincing people to let me help them be great. We talked a little while longer about payment schedules and promotional ideas before wrapping up. "It's going to be great working with you, Ms. Alexander," I said, closing my briefcase and standing.

"I'm looking forward to it. Thanks again for traveling so far. I know our partnership will be worth every bit of the trouble. And, tell Jacob I said hello."

"The pleasure is all mine with coming to meet you." I tried not to pay too much attention to the way her eyes fluttered when she spoke his name. I shrugged it off. I must've been paranoid after seeing him at the club the night before. "I'll most definitely tell him. Is it Ms., or Mrs.?"

"You had it right the first time. I'm single and on the prowl, honey," she said, smiling mischievously. "Ain't none of these men safe around here," Susie said becoming looser than she had been the entire meeting. She winked, running her pale fingers through her curly brown hair as she laughed.

Jacob introduced me to Susie via email as a potential client, so her business referral had come to me through him.

"I hear you. I'll be in touch with you very soon with the final PR plans. Right now, I'd better get going. Thanks again for the business. Have a great day," I said, attempting to keep our relationship all business. I walked to the elevator, wondering if Jacob was banging Susie, too.

When I made it downstairs, Jacob was standing by the exit. Fury raged inside my heart, yet it still skipped a beat upon seeing him. He had this apologetic look on his face, while holding a bouquet of pink roses in his hands.

"Hey Destiny," he said with a smile and enclosed me in his arms. He leaned down, captured my lips, and kissed me without any care that passersby saw us.

His kiss almost made me forget about last night. Almost.

I pulled away from him. "We need to talk," I said, walking over to the nearest bench to sit down.

He walked behind me and slowly sat down. He looked leery of what I was about to say. "Sounds serious, especially when I thought you would be more enthused to see me."

"Oh, I would've been tickled pink to see you last night," I said bluntly. "But that was then. This is now."

"I apologized for that. Why are you so upset?" he said, touching my hand.

I studied every line and contour of the face of the man who sat in my face and pretended I was the one with the issue.

"I saw you," I spat.

"What do you mean?"

"I. Saw. You," I said through clenched teeth.

"Okay, you saw me, but where? And, what about you seeing me is pissing you off," he asked the questions, but his paling complexion showed me that he knew what I was talking about.

"Last night.

"At the lounge?"

"Yes! Who was the girl that was sucking your face?"

Anxiety ran across his face. Hurt entered his eyes. "Her name is Justine," he said as if that was supposed to mean something to me.

"Go on!" I said.

"She's my girlfriend. I mean ex-girlfriend," he continued. "We're just friends, Destiny."

I struggled to process his revelation. Part of me reeled from the news. I half expected him to say she was some girl he met up with and it meant nothing. Or, maybe he got drunk and found himself caught up kissing some random woman. But no. She was *his* woman.

"Girlfriend?" I growled out, as my right hand itched to slap the taste out of his gorgeous mouth.

He nodded. "She's my ex, and we used to live together."

My jaw dropped open.

"She's not just a girlfriend. You lived with her, too. You have got to be kidding me," I hollered as I looked down at the flowers clutched in my hand. I threw them at him and jumped to my feet. "You are a cheater, and that's lower than the lowest piece of shit."

I stomped out the building towards my car. Just as I reached my car, two strong arms encircled me.

"Let me go!" I reached for my door handle and struggled to open it.

"Wait Destiny, listen! Just hear me out, at least."
He held one hand on my door and one on my waist.

"Hear you say what? What exactly could you say to
me, when I saw the chemistry you have with another
woman who you say is your ex? You still love her. She's
your...your... girlfriend!" My heart broke all over
again.

It felt like I was experiencing my divorce again, but
only through Jacob. It was wrong to persecute him
with my past with Montie, but that was how I felt as I
admitted to myself that Jacob had another woman.

"It's over between us, Destiny," he said, his eyes
boring holes into me. "I broke up with her for good last
night."

"Really, so after sucking each other's tongues, you
took her home and told her it's over? You must really
think I'm a fool. It didn't appear that things were
ending last night. Next, you'll be telling me that you
called an overnight U-Haul." I rolled my eyes, and
threw my hands up. "Now, move your hand, so I can
get in my car and leave."

"No. Not until you stop resisting me and fucking
listen."

"What I saw spoke volumes, Jacob. I don't need to
hear anything else."

"She was my best friend before we became lovers. I
have known for a while now that we were not going to

56

last, but she was too unstable to just dump and move on."

I laughed until I doubled over.

"Unstable? Is that really what you are going to tell me about that girl? She didn't look too unstable to me. Did you have sex with her last night?"

"No, I didn't, and it's true," he replied, running his hand through his close cropped, dark hair. "She has tried committing suicide a couple times. When I broke up with her a month ago and moved back into my own house, she began seeing her psychologist again. But last night, she threatened to kill herself again. I was afraid she was going to do it, so I took her out to cheer her up and slept on the sofa. This morning, I told her that I can't keep doing this. I'm not in love with her. I don't think I ever was, but I don't want her suicide on my conscience."

I took a long look at him. Our relationship began on lies, and my heart was starting to wonder if trying to sort out truth from fiction was worth it. My mind was screaming, "Move on." But, he sounded genuine. What if everything he said was correct? How would I handle a suicidal boyfriend with whom I wanted to break up? I wouldn't want a man's death on my conscious either. Yet, I didn't know if I could just get past the way they kissed. There was a fire burning in their union.

"Jacob, I just don't think..." I began.

"Don't think about it anymore. You obviously didn't stick around to see that I pushed her off of me and we left shortly afterwards."

He was right. I didn't stay to watch the freak show.

"Jacob...I..." His strong tongue caressing mine cut off my words. I melted into his embrace, for a moment forgetting why I was even upset. The same feelings I had when we first met came rushing back as he brushed a hand across my cheek.

"Make love to me and you will know it is real," he whispered against our deep and passionate kiss.

"No. I won't be doing that. That's what I won't do, ever again," I whispered the words that he urgently caught between his lips.

"Don't deny me this. I need you. What you saw meant nothing. This means something,'" he urged as he latched his lips onto mine and pulled me closer to him.

"Stop it, Jacob! Just don't..." I held my hand up and pushed him away as hard as I could.

He barely moved an inch. But, he let me go.

"Destiny, you're in here, and no other woman can say that," he pat his shirt over his heart. "Jacob's Destiny..."

"If you feel that way about me, then why did you spend the night with her, instead of me?" I fought hard to walk the fine line between a woman in charge of her feelings and giving in to the moment.

"That's a fair question. And, you deserved better than that. The only reason I can give is that I owed her the proper ending to our once romantic relationship. She was in a very vulnerable place last night and I tried to let her down as easily as I could. However, if you give me another chance, I promise never to put her before you ever again. That's on everything I have in my heart."

My mood softened.

Erratic breaths and pounding heartbeats returned to normal, after he kissed me again. Short of saying that I forgave him, I nodded and climbed into my car. Jacob tapped on the window.

"Where are we headed?" he asked.

"The Embassy," I answered, allowing him back in despite all rationale.

******

One Hour Later

We fell down on my bed, our lips taking over, as his hands caressed my breasts. I moaned, wrapping my arms around him and massaging the nape of his neck. For a brief moment, I knew this was a mistake. It's hard to fight what's wrong in the heat of the moment. Our naked bodies pressed against each other, as we continued the dance between our tongues. His tongue would slide against mine and I would sigh, with a certain urgency filling the room. As the kiss deepened, I felt his hips gyrate sensuously against mine.

"Condom..." he softly murmured, breaking from the kiss.

I pulled him back against me.

"I started the pill," I murmured, ready to get on with the reason we were there.

Again, all rationale was out the window, as he slid inside me bare. I ached for the moment our bodies became one.

He plied into my tender flesh, seemingly more excited about our union than I anticipated. I wondered if it was because the truth was finally out that he had a girlfriend and I was okay with it.

"You feel so good, Destiny," he said, grazing his lips across mine.

"You feel good, too," I moaned, biting his lower lip.

Our bodies continuously glided against one another, as his groans intensified.

"Ahhh..." I screamed, when a violent orgasm rippled through my body. My lower lips gripped his shaft like a vice as he entered and exited.

"Fuck..." he blurted out and crashed down on top of me. Within seconds, his hot seed gushed against my vaginal walls, as if he had been holding out for this moment. He slipped his hands underneath my ass and gripped tight, his lips trailing to my chin, neck, and shoulder. His tongue encased my skin, eager to explore more as he thrust his cock into my tight cunt. "You're so wet. I don't want to stop."

His lips trailed to my breast, circling my nipple and sucking it like he was thirsty for its taste. He bucked as cum seeped from his long shaft into my soft, pink love tunnel. Nothing mattered except the way he dug deeper. I arched my back to allow him even deeper access.

Captivated by the moment, I groaned, while he growled out his satisfaction. "You are so sexy," he whispered in my ear. "I love the way you look naked. Don't you ever deny me the sight."

When he pulled out of me, our bodies remained connected, letting our lips do the talking. I relaxed against his warm breath, as he lowered his mouth to my love canal. He sucked with passion, running his tongue over my clit. I opened my mouth, begging for a breath to escape, but it was as if I had no air left in my lungs.

"Wow..." I sighed, when he dipped his tongue further, moaning against my sensitive flesh.

Somewhere between the depth of his stroke and warmth of his tongue, all worries had vanished.

CHAPTER EIGHT

JACOB

I Love Her, Too

The next morning at the airport, I paid for a ticket just to accompany Destiny to her gate. I strained to say goodbye to her. I kissed her as many times as I could, wanting to kiss away any doubts about Justine from her mind. Given time, I would prove to her that she was my top priority.

"Are you sure you don't want to fly back on my jet?" I asked, wanting to do anything possible to make her comfortable. "It'll be less stressful for you than riding with all of these people, going through baggage claim and all of that," I said, gesturing to the busy airport.

"Awe, that was sweet when you asked me the first five times, but I'll be fine," she said, still in my arms. A beautiful smile flashed across her face. "Do you remember when we first met?" she asked.

"Of course, I do." I remembered every moment exactly the way it was. Meeting women and having sex on the same day wasn't the way I approached relationships, meaningful ones, anyway. However, there was something very different about Destiny and I knew this the moment I laid my eyes on her.

"What do you remember, Jacob?"

"I remember you walking out of Tazi's and bumping into me. Then you looked at me as if I were some kind of god."

She blushed and playfully hit my arm. "Oh, is that how you remember it?"

"Something like that," I said, kissing her again. "You made me feel visible and important, and it wasn't because of my money. Being treated like that was a breath of fresh air. People always treat me nice, but it's hard to tell if it's genuine. Once you get on the plane headed back to Atlanta, I will be missing that in my life."

"I'm going to miss you, too, Jacob. I really enjoyed our time together after I got past everything else." Her eyes wandered away from mine briefly. "I can't wait until we can see each other again."

"I'll be in Atlanta next week. You're not going to make me wait this long to see you again."

"Okay," Destiny submitted. "Jacob, I just want to say that I..." a screeching voice yelling my name cut her off.

"Jacobbbb!" the voice called out again.

I jumped away from Destiny and on guard to protect her. I was pissed when I found the source of the noise.

"Oh, hell! It's Justine," I warned Destiny, while keeping her behind me.

"Excuse me?" she said and stepped around me.

"It's Justine. I don't know why she's here. This is insane." I placed an arm protectively around Destiny's waist. She was my main concern.

"Jacob, I don't want this lady killing herself because of me." Destiny stepped away from me and out of my grasp. "Just tell her we're business associates and you gave me a ride to the airport and that we were sitting here discussing business."

"I'm not lying about who you are to me. Besides, we were hugging," I said, watching Justine walk as fast as she could in her heels trying to reach us.

"Just tell her something that won't have her overdosing by midnight, but please handle her once and for all, Jacob, or I'm out!" Destiny picked up her bags and walked toward her terminal.

"Destiny, wait..."

The shock of Justine rushing toward me stopped me from chasing after Destiny. Justine's ass was bat-shit crazy for following us there.

"What?" Destiny answered, curtly. Her soft facial features were stern.

I went to her. "I want you to listen to this so you will not have mixed feelings about us."

"I had to buy a damn plane ticket to get back here and find out you're cheating on me with...with *her*,

Jacob? I thought you said you were going to your mother's church this morning. What the hell are you doing here in the airport, all hugged up with this black...bitch?" Justine spat out when she reached me.

After she insulted my woman, all of that protect her feelings shit was out. Destiny's face was full of hurt, and I wasn't having any of it.

"Justine, we've been friends for a long time, and we shared a lot, but you are crossing a very serious line by insulting my woman. If you ever find it necessary to address her, it's beautiful black queen to you," I said, stepping close to her, pissed the hell off. "You need to calm your stupid-acting spoiled ass down," I added.

"You're defending her, Jacob?" Justine asked, incredulous.

"She is my girlfriend; of course, I'm defending her. You just watch what you say about her," I said with Destiny standing close by.

A vacant look entered Justine's eyes. Her voice flattened as she said, "Jacob, why are you doing this to me?"

"Justine, we talked about this just this morning."

"I know what we talked about, but you're all I have. I can't handle losing you. If you don't want me, I have no reason to live," she said.

Justine removed a bottle of pills from her pocket. She opened it and began pouring the contents down her throat.

"Justine, don't swallow those pills," I said rushing to put my hand out in front of her mouth. "Spit them out now."

Her eyes were defiant. She shook her head vigorously, and a pained look entered her eyes as tears flowed down her cheeks.

"I'm here for you, Justine. You have to know that I'm not ever leaving your side. Now, spit those pills out," I said for the sake of her life.

"But you have left my side," Justine cried as she spat the pills onto the floor. Her voice went from calm to yelling within seconds.

"I'll always be your friend. We just can't be more than that." I didn't know what else I could do to help her. I wasn't going to lead her on by telling her what she wanted to hear, though.

"No, because you've been fucking around with Destiny since you went to Atlanta last month. That's why you're not into me anymore. I went through your phone and read the sweet messages you send to her. You never sent things like that to me. She's the reason you think you want to leave me. She's taking you away!"

"I'm not taking anything," Destiny said.

"Ouuhh! Don't talk to me at all," Justine screamed at Destiny. "He's just fulfilling a fantasy with you."

"Stop that, Justine. The way I feel about Destiny is deeper than anything you'll understand," I admitted.

"Oh, I understand that she means enough for you to flaunt her around Miami. In Miami, Jacob, really?" Justine started wailing like a baby. Her shoulders shook violently as she sobbed and made a scene. People who were once whisking by us had stopped and stared to make sure the irate woman was okay. One older lady pulled out her cell phone and was pointing at her. Security would be in my business in no time.

I felt a swift kick in the gut when I looked around and Destiny was gone. I grabbed Justine's arm and pulled her toward the exit.

"If you make me lose her with your outbursts, you will regret it," I warned.

"Are you threatening me, Jacob?" she asked and touched my hand covering her arm.

"It's a promise that you won't like the results of pushing that woman out of my life. Now, for the final time, it's over between us." I moved her hand and stormed toward the drop-off zone. After this stunt, a clean break from Justine was necessary.

CHAPTER NINE

DESTINY

Breathe Again

The tick-tock sound of the clock on the wall got on my last nerve. I had yet to replace the clock with one that made less noise. The aggravating sound kept me company at night. My little rug rats had abandoned me to spend the weekend with a family friend who had kids their age, so I was all alone. According to the clock, it was three in the morning. I couldn't sleep. I just kept remembering seeing Jacob console Justine at the airport.

She showed up looking even more beautiful than when I caught them making out at the lounge. Standing there in a peach Sunday dress and black and peach stiletto heels, she had a look of victory on her face when Jacob told her, *"I'm here for you, Justine. You have to know that I'm not ever leaving your side..."*

He had searched my eyes for understanding when he said it. I understood that he was attempting to get her to lower the pill bottle. He appeared torn as he looked from me to Justine, so I looked away, allowing him to make his choice without interference. He said what he felt necessary to calm Justine down, but the possibility of him never leaving her side cut like a knife. Was he also discarding the love we made just hours before? Our passion seemed so real, and he was willing to wipe it away with his dedication to Justine.

"I'm...Never...Leaving...Your...Side." I thought about the way I felt, when I slowly walked onto my plane with those words repeating in my mind. I felt weak.

"Jacob," I had said, just above a murmur. *"Jacob, how could you stand here and chose her, again?"*

Mama used to say, 'Just because a man's organ is inside of you, doesn't mean he's into you,' and she's always right. Hot tears flowed down my face as I recounted every second of that weekend that started and ended with rejection. The symptoms of losing Jacob waxed and waned through my soul. He hadn't called in the past two weeks, and I couldn't bring myself to dial his number. I meditated and prayed that I could get him, and the dysfunction that came along with him, out of my system, and fast.

As I lay in bed half asleep, half thinking, I heard the faint sound of my name and a knock. I froze still under my mocha colored comforter. It hadn't been the first time I'd awoken to hear what I thought was a knock at the door, or someone calling my name. I figured it was only my mind playing tricks on me.

The clock continued to make the tick-tock, tick-tock noise until I fell into a state of sub-consciousness. Then, the knock happened again. This time, there were three knocks, a pause, and another. I don't know how, but I could tell by the rhythm of the beat that it was Jacob.

I pulled my tired body from underneath the covers, walked slowly to my bedroom door, and took a suspicious glance down the hallway. Not a single soul had ever come to my door in the middle of the night unexpected. I should have been scared since I had nothing but a knife to protect myself, but I was calm. If Jacob were to be on my doorstep, there would be no way I could protect myself from him. Like a thief in the night, he would steal my heart. The last thing I needed was a temptation as sweet as Jacob was. A midnight visit from him would not be good, and I had to think about my well-being.

Three more knocks, a pause, and another knock brought me out of my room and up the hall. The sound wasn't a dream, and my mind wasn't playing tricks on me. I was wide awake.

My feet had just sunk into the plush carpet in the foyer when I heard a man's voice. "Destiny, open the door. I know you're in there. Please, baby," he said before doing his signature knock again.

I looked out the window and froze where I stood. Jacob Turner was indeed at my door. I turned on my heels to go open the door and stopped cold as memories washed over me. As much as I had to say to him, I was a bundle of nerves.

Fully aware of one hundred and one reasons not to let him inside my home, I walked to the foyer and punched in the security code to disarm the house. I unlatched several locks and opened the door.

"I miss you," he said, and before the door closed, our lips met. Trailing kisses from my neck down to my chest, he kept repeating, "I'm sorry. I'm sorry. I'm so sorry for doing you wrong."

Get your fucking lips off me! How dare you come in here kissing on me with the same lips you kissed Justine's ass? That's what I thought I said. Instead, I silently stood by, as he took control of every part of me, pulling me close, caressing my body, putting my mind at ease.

He didn't say I love you with his lips. His spirit spoke it into mine. I was completely under his spell as I closed the door behind him. My clothes fell from my body in fluid subconscious movements. My fingers went to his boxers and I removed them with ease. I needed to feel him again, no matter at what cost. I dragged him down the hallway into my bedroom, and we fell onto the bed, our lips caressing every inch of one another's body.

"Damn, I missed you so much," he growled against my neck before moving his lips down the long length of my right arm. He captured my fingers in his mouth and sucked diligently at the digits.

I sighed, while closing my eyes to all the painful memories. I blocked out anything that would stop the amazing sex I knew we would have, the amazing sex we always had.

I gripped onto his shoulders and flipped him over, so that I was on top. He wasn't the only one able to take charge. I eased down his body and lowered my mouth to his enlarged erection. Our eyes connected as he let out a slow brush of air from his lips. I lowered my lips and swirled my tongue around his swollen tip.

He groaned as I teasingly brushed the tip of my tongue down the length of his shaft slowly. Hearing his moans as he moved beneath me, I smiled to myself and relished his murmuring. I glided my tongue to the other side of his erection, slowly easing up his shaft. He hummed his pleasure when I captured him in my mouth.

"Fuck..." he groaned, as I took him all the way in. His hard rod pulsed against my tongue, and I knew he wouldn't be able to hold it any longer. "Ugh..." he groaned and tried to pull back.

"Give me all that cum, Jacob," I said, as I licked and sucked his shaft until he released a load onto my lips and mouth. I sucked him with hunger, swallowing every morsel of his release.

"Damn it, I love you," he said and grasped my hair, slowly lifting my head from his lap.

His lips crashed down upon mine, and we passionately kissed, embracing the moment. I straddled him and he entered me with a smooth force, showing me that there was no doubt that he was now in command, but being gentle about it.

"Do you love me, or do you love making love to me?" I asked, as his lips left my fingers and traveled back up to mine.

"You," he groaned, momentarily breaking his invasive kiss and relishing in the fact that we were one. Our tongues massaged one another, frantically searching for an escape. His cock pounded hard into my tight canal, and I gripped his throbbing manhood within my walls. He flipped me over and took total control.

"Ah," I whimpered, digging my nails into his creamy skin as he entered me again. I held onto his back, pressing him closer to me, as his dick went where no man had ever gone before, so deep inside. "Please..." I sighed, before he unloaded his seed inside me.

His guttural groans sent sensations through my body. He lifted his lips to mine, as his hips bucked fiercely against mine.

"Baby..." he moaned between his tender kisses.

74

"Yes?"

"Don't ever leave me," he commanded, after he crashed onto the bed beside me and pulled me close to him.

I truly was lost in the moment, and that happened each time we were together. I closed my eyes and sighed. I pulled myself up on an elbow to look at him. He had a gratifying grin on his sexy lips. Jacob could have been there only for another romp session, with plans to go back to Justine tomorrow. I shook my head, as if shaking it would erase what we'd just shared, and we could start over with him knocking on the door.

"Why are you here, Jacob?"

"What do you mean, why am I here? I needed you," he said.

"You haven't called me since I left Miami. I thought you decided to work it out with Justine. Why are you dragging me back into the middle of your mess? I can't deal with you and her again, Jacob." I pushed back a tear that was threatening to fall. "Please leave now."

"After what just happened here? You don't mean that," he said touching my arm. "You are not a woman that a man just gets up and walks away from."

I looked at the messy sheets and nodded. "Yes, we had sex, and yes, I enjoyed it. I'll always enjoy it, but Jacob, I don't want this on one minute, off the next, fling that's happening. I don't deserve to be treated like some whore you screw when you're in the mood, or until Justine throws a temper tantrum and threatens to fake kill herself. "

"I know you deserve more, Destiny. I'm here to give it to you."

I started to get out of bed.

He reached for my hand. "Hear me out," he said with a pained look on his face.

I threw my hands in the air. "Fine. Talk."

"I did go to her house after we left the airport that day. She tried to convince me to stay with her and that our friendship meant so much more than us, but the only image I could see was you. Your smile interrupted my thoughts in the middle of our conversation. Thoughts of your sexy brown thighs would rush through my mind in the middle of a conference call, while at work. The more I tried to imagine things the way they were before I met you, the more I realized that could never be. I need you in my life. Give me a chance to make it right."

"You really hurt me, Jacob, but I knew what I was getting into when we got in bed the first day I met you. The minute I saw you kissing Justine, I should've never allowed you into my bed again. I should've moved on. I had no business sleeping with you then and I have no business sleeping with you now."

"But yet, you can't resist it."

"It'll never happen again."

"Don't say that, when you know it's not true. You may think us sleeping together on the first day made me look at you differently, but it didn't. We didn't know each other, but our kindred energy undeniably pulled us together."

"You're charming and handsome. What woman wouldn't have great energy with you? That doesn't make any of it right, Jacob."

"But that's just it. What we have *is* right. I love you, and I'm not the type of man to go around proclaiming my love to every woman I meet. Look, I'm done with Justine. I'm really done. I only have feelings for *you*."

"You're not worried that she's going to kill herself?" I asked, rolling my eyes away from him.

"I thought about that, but I have to be true to the way I feel. I have to believe that she'll be alright without me."

Still unconvinced, I huffed and crossed my arms. "I don't know, Jacob."

"Let me do something nice for you...take you somewhere special. Anywhere you want to go. I'll give you anything you want, as long as you give me you," he said, kissing his way up my back and to my neck. "I need you tonight...and every night."

"What about in the daytime?" I teased.

"Night and day," he answered.

"This is too much..."

"Only if you make it," he said, continuing to kiss every inch of my body.

"I didn't expect you to come here. We can't figure this all out tonight," I said, holding back the tremble in my voice.

"I don't want to figure it all out tonight. I just want you to let me do this to you," he said, pulling me toward him for another earthshaking kiss.

I broke free before things got too heated. "My heart, alone, is not enough to get us through this."

"What if my heart is big enough for both of us?" he said, kissing me again. He looked so genuine I felt vulnerable when he caressed me. "I'm with you one hundred percent. Even if you send me away from here tonight, I'll be back tomorrow. I'm not going anywhere."

"That's the same thing you told Justine."

"Well, I'm telling you now; and not because you're threatening to kill yourself, but because a part of me will die without you."

"That's kind of deep," I said. "Let's just take this slow and see how things play out, Jacob."

"They'll play out better than you expect, trust me. I have my ways of showing you," he said, lying down beside me.

I thought for a second. "So did you use "your ways" to find out where I live?"

"Like I said, I have my ways," he said. His neatly shaven beard had grown so much since the last time I saw him.

"Humph," I said. "You better not be having me followed."

"Maybe," he joked and I hit his arm. "Nah, I sweet-talked Susie Alexander into giving me your address. You know she has a thing for me, so it was kind of easy," he said, running his hand across his beard.

"You probably did more than sweet talking," I said, regretting rolling my eyes, crossing my arms and saying the words as soon as I'd said them. Unwanted thoughts roamed through my mind. I could imagine him having sex with Susie on the same desk I signed her contract on.

He must have sensed my insecurity. He pulled me into his arms and said, "I have not had sexual relations with that woman."

I laughed at his attempt to be funny. "Uh huh."

"But I would have walked to the end of the earth to get your address and surprise you. Now, kiss me again."

I turned my head in defiance.

"Come on, baby, don't deny me those juicy lips," he said with a devastatingly sexy look in his hazel green eyes. He leaned in and sucked tenderly on my neck, and his cologne tickled my senses like cool air.

Where was Tasha when I needed her? I needed that coochie intervention at the very moment he began to beg. Having a will of their own, my full lips puckered and moved toward his. Our lips met and embraced as we lay in the center of my bed. I slipped away, and we gravitated together. All I could do was say an internal prayer for mercy on my soul.

"You can have me, if that's what you want," I whispered.

"Need," he moaned into my mouth, and in one quick swoop, Jacob was on top of me. He took one of my breasts into his mouth and sucked ever so gently on my tender bud. "You taste sweet. I want to taste all of you." He moved down to my thighs and I tensed.

"Relax babe," he said climbing back up to kiss my lips.

"How long do you plan to be in town?" I asked.

"For as long as you want me."

"So I guess that means you'll be here to go with me to church in the morning?" I asked, as his hand eased under me to embrace the small of my back.

"Church?"

"Yes, you know the building where people go pray and learn scripture."

"Yeah," he pulled me as close as our bodies could get. "Whatever you want."

"Fine, then…" I squirmed from underneath him and sat on the edge of the bed. "I want you to come back in the morning so we can go to church."

"But baby, technically, it's already morning," he said, gesturing to the sunrise attempting to shine through the curtains.

"I know, but I'm going to need you to come back when I've had more time to check my emotions."

Getting out of bed, I reached down, picked up his trail of clothes and threw them at him. I then left my room and waited in the living room, as he got dressed. It wasn't long before he was heading my way.

"If this is what you want, I'll do it, but it's hard to walk out this door." He paused, looking at me as if he wanted me to respond. "I'll be back later today," he said, as I stood holding the door open.

"See you then," I responded, avoiding his gaze.

"Destiny?"

"Yes?"

"I love you." He walked out the door and I shut the door behind him, forcing myself not to watch him walk down the driveway and to his car.

CHAPTER TEN

DESTINY

After the Pain

The next morning, I awoke to the scrumptious scent of our sex, filling my bedroom. Jacob was an expert lover, and the essence of his love lingered as a pleasant memory. While I would have loved to lay there and think about our lovemaking, the fact that Justine had been an obvious wedge just a few weeks ago had my attention as well. I pushed back the comfortable covers and wiped the sleep from my eyes.

Getting out of bed, the first thing I did was walk to my vanity. I took a long look in the mirror. I assessed the woman that stared back at me. Observing the undeniable glow covering me, shining like headlights through my eyes that had been puffy, I knew what my decision was going to be. If Jacob proved to be truly over Justine, I would give us a chance.

A chance to be Jacob's Destiny, I thought as I walked over to my wardrobe and pulled out a nice, pink Sunday dress to wear. It was a shirt dress with a slim black belt. I found matching black and pink open-toe stilettos, and a fancy black and pink church hat Mama gave me last year.

An hour later, I was fully dressed and standing in the doorway talking to Jacob. He made it to my house before I called to remind him about church. He dressed in a pair of black slacks and a polo shirt with accents of pink. His black crocodile loafers and designer shades went perfectly with his cool, sophisticated look.

"You look wonderful, Destiny," he stated, as we walked hand in hand to his car.

"You look quite debonair yourself," I said before stopping in my tracks to give him a once over, "Thanks for going to church with me."

"I haven't been inside a church in years, and had no intention of going today, but for you—anything. All you have to do is say the word and I'm," he looked intently into my eyes, before spinning me around observing every contour of my body, "where you want me to be."

Smiling, he took my hand and we continued the walk to the car. I reached for the door handle and dropped my hands to my side when I caught his glare. "Don't you dare touch that door, not as long as I'm present," he said, opening the door.

"Yes sir," I said with a nod.

We filled the ride to the church with conversation, catching up on personal and business life. We hadn't had a chance to talk over the past few weeks, so he let me know that the Wyoming office opening was a success.

"Yeah, we did our ribbon cutting in the forty-ninth state," he beamed with pride when he explained. "Opening that location is all I have been able to eat and breath lately."

"I'm happy for you. Your grandfather would be so proud, Jacob."

I could tell he was thinking about his grandfather and wondering what he would have thought about the new location.

"This is what he wanted. I'm honored that my father and I are keeping his legacy alive," he said.

"That really is an honor." I squeezed his hand.

"Now that most of my big goals are so close to being accomplished, I can work on my biggest goal." He brought my hand up to his lips and kissed my ring finger.

"Last night, you said you'd be in town for as long as I wanted you here. What did you mean by that?"

"I gave it a lot of thought when you left Miami. My grandmother is growing older and my mother doesn't need to be traveling to Atlanta all the time to take care of her. You are here. I have offices in Atlanta. All roads lead here…to you."

"Are you saying that you're moving to Atlanta?"

"I already bought a condo. All I need is decorating. I was hoping you could help me with that; that's if you don't have a problem with me being in your city," he teased.

"I have no problem with it at all. I just want you to do what you want, and not something on an impulse that will end up making you miserable."

"I'll be fine here," he said as the GPS directed him to turn right to St. Margaret Baptist Church. We pulled into the church parking lot and parked. He took off his seatbelt. His eyes devoured me whole, as he looked at me. "Make no mistake about it, you, alone, are worth the move," he said, took my chin into his hands and pulled my face to his for one of his signature passionate kisses.

I released myself from my seatbelt and wrapped my arms tightly around his neck, deepening our kiss. We sat there enthralled by the magic of our connection as his hands, which had so securely held my face, moved down to my waist. I had no doubt, that he would have pulled me into his lap right there in that church parking lot, if the construct of his car didn't stop him.

"We'd better go inside," I said, noticing Mrs. Tyler pull up beside us and stare over her brown, rimmed glasses. Her grandson was looking out of the window with a big smile on his face.

Jacob released my waist and rubbed his hands over the burgeoning erection in his pants.

I smiled at Mrs. Tyler and waved. She waved back and placed her oversized red, church hat atop her flowing ringlet curls. The pudgy woman got out of her car with her cheesing grandson in tow, and briskly walked up the church steps, looking back at our car every few seconds with condemnation. Between her being nosey and Jacob's protruding erection, I shook my head and turned away coyly to fix my makeup in his passenger mirror.

"Well... uh, give me a few minutes to get myself together, and then I'll go in with you. Or, I can catch up later," he said.

"No, I'll wait," I said, giving his thigh a reassuring rub. "I want us to walk in together."

"Babe, if you touch me like that again, we will not make it inside that church today. And for the time being, look out of the window, so your beautiful face won't excite me."

We laughed.

"Come on. Let's go in, or we'll be late," I said, reaching for my door handle a few minutes later.

His penetrating glare warned me not to touch the handle. He got out and rushed around to open my door. Glowing, we walked hand in hand into the church and sat in the fifth pew. I spoke to members I knew and gave nods to others.

The sermon was about faithfulness and the pastor was going hard on the message. I gave Jacob's hand a squeeze and he put his arm around me. We took in the riveting delivery of the biblical message. I hoped it would stay with us, because we needed all the faith we could get.

When we left church that day, Jacob promised, "Destiny, as long as I'm with you, I'll never choose another woman over you again. I'm all yours."

"The past is the past. As long as you do right by me and, when the time is right, my kids, I'm all in," I confessed my feelings to him.

Relief marched across his face. "You don't know how much it means for me to hear you say that, Destiny. I will spend as long and as much as it takes to make up for our rocky start."

CHAPTER ELEVEN

DESTINY

No Time Like the Present

He meant those words. The days my kids were with their father, he stayed at my house and we began to connect fully. I was falling even more in love with him and felt his love flowing over me. We were becoming a great union and I didn't want that to end.

"When do your kids come home?" he asked me, kissing me softly on the lips.

I lowered myself to his body and rested my chin on his chest. Our eyes locked together.

"Tomorrow and it's going to be a sweet day, when I see my babies again. I miss them." I smiled at Jacob. "And, I can't wait for them to meet you."

"I can't wait to meet them," he spoke, causing my smile to widen. "Whenever you're ready, that is."

Though I felt it would be perfect to get them together, the timing needed to be right. Montie Jr. and Montana had yet to come to grips with their father having a separate home. They weren't ready to see me with another man.

"It'll be soon," I replied and pulled myself up.

"Soon?" He asked, grabbing me around my waist and flipping me over.

I giggled as he nibbled playfully on my ear. He held my hands over my head, pressed down to the bed. His lips went to my neck and he fervently sucked my skin.

"Very soon, Jacob..." I whined, moving underneath him, trying to get my hands free from his grip.

He wouldn't listen. He nipped at my chin a few times before trailing kisses down to my neck and chest. "How soon?" He was relentless in his movements, circling his teeth around my nipples.

"Oh God, Jacob..." I moaned, trying desperately to break from his hold. "Ugh..." I let out a deep sigh. Wetness pooled between my thighs, and I itched to have him inside me.

His tongue surrounded my breasts. He glided up to my lips, and I latched onto him, taking in the wonderful taste that was all Jacob. He shifted to push his ever-rising erection inside of my wetness. My hands remained pinned down, so all I could do was scream when he penetrated me.

"Ahhh..."

His hips moved against mine. His lips forcibly took over my mouth. His body crashed against mine over and over.

Blown away, I finally gave up on having my hands free and just went with it. That's when the faint sound of my cell phone ringing interrupted the moment. I tensed and looked down at my phone, but his pounding into my aching pussy was enough to keep me in place.

Jacob moved fluidly inside of me until I floated away to ecstasy. I groaned deep within, when he gave one last thrust and his cum ravished my hole.

"Oh, Destiny, you're so good, baby," he growled, jerking against me with his forceful thrusts. His ragged breathing accompanied a scowl of pleasure on his face.

"Holy shit," I breathed out, falling back against the bed as an orgasm rendered me too weak to do anything else. "You...a...maze...me!"

"You amaze me more," he replied, kissing me gently on the corner of my lip and then covering my mouth.

My tongue slid inside, slowly and meaningfully. As I was about to deepen the kiss, I heard my phone ring out a text message. My eyes opened and I stared at him.

"Don't you dare move," he rasped out.

"It could be my kids."

He released me.

I reached down to the floor where the phone had fallen, when we recklessly tore each other's clothes off.

"Who is it?" he asked.

"Montie," I answered as I read his text message.

Montie: Hey, I hope you're home. I'm on my way over with the kids. I got called out of town for a meeting that I can't miss. Be there in about ten minutes.

I stared at the phone, rereading the message.

"Get dressed. The kids are on their way home."

Jacob rolled over and sat on the edge of the bed. "Do you want me to leave?"

I read Montie's message again.

"No, you don't have to leave. I'd be honored for you to meet my children."

****

Jacob watched attentively as I moved about the kitchen, preparing for Montie Jr. and Montana's homecoming. Ever so often, I'd catch his eyes drifting to my waist or admiring my breasts. That was flattering, but, when our gaze found one another's, it lingered with understanding. I was in love with him, and I was ready for whatever came next.

By the time Montie knocked on the door, I was pulling a muffin pan out of the oven. I made twenty-four piping hot, delicious cupcakes for my little lovelies. I walked past Jacob and touched his arm. "This is a big step for us. Are you sure, you're ready to take it? You could always make a quick exit out the back door and meet them when you are ready."

"Come on, Destiny. Do I look like the kind of man that runs out the back door?"

"No, you don't."

"Okay, let's do this."

We walked to the door and I opened it. Montie Jr. rushed through the door dressed like a little Transformer. He dropped his Transformers book bag in the foyer, and hugged me.

"Mommy! I missed you this much." He stretched his little, five-year-old arms far and wide.

"Mommy, me miss you much, too," Montana said in her toddler talk, stretching her arms like her brother. She was wearing a pink sundress with an oversized yellow ribbon shaped like the sun. Her wavy hair had a matching yellow ribbon, pulling it into a huge ponytail.

I hugged my lovelies close and said, "Mommy missed you too! Go put your bags up and then go to the kitchen. I have a surprise for you."

The kids scurried away with Montie Jr. in the lead. He did stop halfway to his room and look at his sister, and then went back to help her with her bag. He was such the little gentleman. Ever since I divorced his father, he'd been my little man of the house.

"Hi," Montie Sr. said, rushing in with his cell phone in one hand and Montana's pink, polka dot overnight bag in the other. Just like when we were married, he had one hundred things on his agenda, and none of them included our family. He barely looked at me, much less Jacob, who was standing to the side observing our interaction. "As you can see, they both are wearing their favorite..." Montie started to say something but paused.

He put his phone back up to his ear and glared at Jacob.

"Let me call you back," Montie told the person on the other end and hung up. He erected his stance, showing off his broad muscles as a result of relentless gym workouts. "Excuse my manners. I'm Montie Brown, the father of Destiny's children, and the owner of this house. And you are?" he reached his hand out to Jacob for a shake.

"I'm Jacob Turner," Jacob said shaking Montie's hand.

"My boyfriend," I added firmly. "And this is not your house!" I fired back.

I was livid that Montie would even think of introducing himself as the owner of my house. We settled every detail of our assets in court, so whatever trick he was trying to pull wasn't coming off as cute.

Montie looked at me as if I was the one who'd lost her mind. "I know whose house this is, Destiny," he shot back.

"So you do remember the details of our divorce?" I asked him.

"I do, and you are correct that you were awarded our house. Still doesn't change the fact that we built it together," he said loud and clear.

For the life of me, I couldn't understand why Montie was acting like a drama king. He wasn't the type to throw around his emotions.

"I'm sure there are some beautiful memories in this house. That's evident by your two children who're in the kitchen, ready to put the icing on those cupcakes you cooked, baby," Jacob said to me, but it was more of a shot at Montie. He took command of the conversation and, like an expert captain, steered us out of an impending shipwreck.

"You're right, honey," I said with a pat on Jacob's arm. "Thank you for reminding me of what's important. You can see yourself out, Montie. I'm not about to argue with our children in the next room. Have a safe trip," I tossed over my shoulder.

Montie fumed out of the house mumbling about how we would talk about this later.

"Thanks," I told Jacob as I lifted Montana up to the sink to wash her hands.

"No problem," Jacob said, waving me off. "I'm here for you now. It's time Montie learned that, too."

"Rub your hands together and wash them good," I said to Montana. Seeing the happiness in her eyes and a smile spread across her chubby, brown cheeks, erased all thoughts of Montie.

Montie Jr. used the step stool to wash his hands, and I sat two of the cupcakes on plates and placed them on the table in front of them. Then, I put the jar of icing on the table and watched as my two youngins' clumsily applied topping to their cupcakes.

"Mommy, who is your friend?" Montie Jr. asked, reminding me that I hadn't formally introduced them.

"Oh, this is Mr. Jacob. He is one of mommy's close friends."

"Ah ya' nice?" Montana asked, licking her icing-filled fingers.

"I will be to you," Jacob said as he walked over to her. He stooped down so that they were the same height. "Are you nice?" he asked.

"I not nice to scrangers, but I nice to you." Montana immediately went back to the routine of dipping her hand into the icing and then cleaning it off by sucking her fingers.

"Well, that's good, because I don't plan to be a stranger long. How about this? Finish your snack and we can go out to the park," Jacob said.

"Yay!" Junior said, squirming in his seat, which caused his little sister to do the same.

"Okay, the park it is!" Jacob said, and then out of the kid's earshot said, "I'm glad my first meeting with your ex-husband blew over with just a few words. I would hate to have Junior and Montana's first thought of me as someone who ripped their father to shreds."

"That would be terrible. I'm glad you knew what to say, because he drives me nuts! We hadn't had one single exchange of words like that since the divorce.

Now, when he sees I have someone over here, he wants to come out of his mouth with some craziness."

"I don't blame him. I'd lose my shit if I knew another man was putting his hands on you, too. It's a man thing."

"He should have known what he had when he had it."

"That's his loss. Now that I have you, I'm going to show him that he messed up royally, and he'll want to reclaim his territory, but it's not going to happen." Jacob placed his arm protectively around my waist.

"Is that what you're doing now, reclaiming your territory?"

"I'm building territory with you. Our foundation has to be strong, because I want this to be forever," he said, as breeze blew through the kitchen window, causing me to rub my shoulders.

"Man, it's getting chilly," I said as Jacob reached over me and closed the window. "It's breezy out there. Are you sure you want to go to the park?" I asked.

"I told Montana I was going to take her to the park. I have to be a man of my word," he said, and I thought any man that had my daughter's best interest at heart was a keeper.

We went to the park that evening. We got on the swings, merry-go-round, and sliding board, right alongside the kids. All four of us laughed, ran and played until there was no energy left in our bones.

When we made it back to my house, I got Montana and Junior bathed and in bed. I plopped down on the sofa beside Jacob, exhausted.

He had his phone in his hand, watching a seminar on finance for construction. I didn't even have the energy to ask him if it was any good.

I laid my head on his shoulder, and within minutes, my heavy eyes closed and I was sound asleep.

CHAPTER TWELVE

DESTINY

It's Okay

When I woke up the next morning, I was in the middle of my bed with my nightclothes on...alone. Somehow, Jacob managed to take me into my bedroom, dress me, and get me into bed. I smiled at his choice of an oversized Tweetie Bird gown. I heard the TV in the living room playing cartoons, which let me know Junior was up.

I stretched and yawned before getting out of bed. As I walked past my vanity heading to the bathroom, I saw a note from Jacob telling me he had an awesome time with the kids and that he would call me later.

After using the bathroom, I went into the living room and gave Junior a big peck on the cheek. I checked in on Montana and she was sleeping soundly. She was a sleepy head, just like me. I went into the kitchen to cook breakfast.

"Mommy, I need to talk to you," Junior said as he walked in the kitchen behind me.

"Sure Montie Jr. What's up, honey?"

Standing three feet away from me, he looked like a little businessman about to present a proposal. He looked so much like Montie, naming him after his father was appropriate.

"It's about Mr. Jacob."

I faced him. "Okay, what about him?"

"Is he your boyfriend?"

"Yes, he is."

"Why didn't I know about him 'til we came home yesterday?"

"Because it wasn't time for you to meet him yet."

"And now it's time."

"Yes."

"Where you meet him at?"

"Downtown at Tazi's."

"He like Tazi's?" Junior asked, as if he finally found common ground with Jacob.

"Yes, he does now. The day we met was his first time there."

"Mommy, he likes Tazi. He likes you. He's nice. I like him."

"I'm glad you do. He really is a good person, but I want you to know that you and Montana are my first loves. No one is more important than you."

Junior walked over and hugged my neck. "It's okay if Jacob be one of your loves, too. I just hope daddy won't be mad."

"My young man, don't worry about that. Your dad will be fine. Go and wash your hands for breakfast and wake your sister up too."

Junior giggled. "She doesn't ever want to get up, not even for breakfast."

He skipped down the hall to get Montana, and I shook my head. That boy was becoming more and more of a man each day.

CHAPTER THIRTEEN

DESTINY

Bridled Passion

Jacob decided that we needed to plan another day out where the kids could just be themselves and continue to get to know him better. I was all for the idea of another family day out. He picked us up right on time, and when I opened the door, he pulled me into a breathtaking kiss.

"Eww," Montana said.

I reluctantly drew back and turned to see her watching us with her hand over her mouth. "Go get your brother," I said. Montana bounded out of the foyer headed to find Junior.

Jacob laughed and rested his hand against his chest.

I turned to him and grinned. "Are you sure you know what you're getting yourself into?"

"I think I can handle it." He leaned in, brushing another kiss against my lips.

"I bet you can." I smiled, knowing he could handle us.

My kids came to the door.

"Are you ready to go bowling?" Jacob clapped his hands together and asked.

"Yes!" They clapped with enthusiasm.

"Let's go then!" Jacob held open the door and we all walked out of the house. My kids and I walked toward my car. "Where are you going?" he asked.

"To my car."

"No, we'll go in my car."

"But mine already has the car seats in it," I protested.

"We'll be fine, Destiny. I had two car seats delivered and put in for the kids today."

"You did what?" I asked, and my question was answered when he opened the door to a black-on-black Bentley SUV that had two leather child seats installed in the back. "Well, okay," I humped my shoulders. "We'll ride with you."

Junior got into the booster seat while Jacob buckled in Montana. I couldn't have asked for anything more, as I laughed at him struggling to buckle her in. He pulled away and closed the door, looking at me.

"What's so funny?" he asked intrigued.

"Isn't too easy, is it?"

"Give me some time. I'm sure I'll get used to it." He got into the driver's side and drove us to the bowling alley.

Junior and Montana mumbled to each other. I'm not sure about what. I glanced in the rearview mirror and watched them, but didn't interrupt. When I returned my attention to Jacob, he was smiling at me. "I'm glad we're doing this," I told him.

He reached over and grabbed my hand, holding it tightly. "Me too," he spoke with the pleasing smile that never left his face.

When he parked, we got out and each of us grabbed one of the kids' hand. Their eyes got big as saucers when they looked at the large building.

"Ever been bowling before, Junior?" Jacob asked.

Junior shook his head without breaking his gaze from the building.

Jacob grabbed my hand. "I rented the entire alley for us today, and lunch will be served in a couple of hours," he announced just before we reached the front counter.

"Jacob, you didn't have to do that. I could have paid for mine..." I began, but he put up a finger to stop me.

"I got this babe. I'm going to show you so much more than this, so get used to it." He winked at me, checked in with the attendant, and led us to alley number three. "Besides, this day is about us. I didn't want anyone else to be in here."

My heart swelled. I felt like royalty. We'd only been together a few months, and he was doing more than my ex had done in four years. It was never about the money. It was always about having his time and being made to feel like I mattered.

"At least let me get our shoes, Jacob."

"Ask for the ones I ordered," he said as I walked away.

"Okay," I said and went to the shoe booth. I grabbed the shoes for everyone and came back to our lane. I put new shoes on Montana, and they fit perfectly. Jacob helped Junior by tying his shoes for him. "You know we could have worn the shoes from the alley. You didn't have to order new ones especially for us. Our feet are not too good to share with the general public," I told him as I laced mine.

"What did I just say, woman?" he said without offering any further explanation. He shook his head as he typed in our names into the computer. "I see you're going to have to get used to how I do things, and it damn sure isn't conventional."

"You're right," I relented. "I'm in for quite a few surprises with you, Mr. Turner."

"Good that you recognize that. Now, enjoy the ride," he winked then his expression turned serious as he looked at the kids. "Okay, the object of the game is to win. We are playing boys vs. girls, and of course the boys will win this thing."

"Yes!" Junior yelled, giving Jacob a high five. He then turned to us and there was a new light in his eyes.

Junior pumped his fists in the air as he sang his battle cry. "Mommy, you both don't stand a chance."

I crossed my arms. "Those are fighting words, son."

Jacob laughed as our eyes met. "The boy is right. We're going to clobber you two," Jacob added.

"We'll see about that," I blurted back.

"Let me show you how to do this, Junior. Stand right here," Jacob picked up the ball and Junior stood next to him watching intently.

"Now, what you have to do is put the ball down behind this white line, and then push it as hard as you can," Jacob said.

He put a lightweight ball down in front of Junior and Junior rolled it. It was a kiddie aisle so the ball went toward the gutter a few times, but the bumpers kept knocking it back out. The ball got to the end and knocked down seven pins.

"Yay, did I win?" Junior asked excitedly.

"You get one more roll, but you're doing great, buddy!" Jacob said, as he and Junior high-fived.

Again, Junior rolled the ball. This time, he knocked down three pins and jumped up and down. "Yes!" He turned to me and his grin was huge. "Mommy, did you see that?"

"I saw it. Great job!" I beamed.

"Your mother is right. That's a good first try," Jacob added.

"Thank you, Mr. Jacob!" Junior threw his arms around Jacob's leg.

"You're welcome!" Jacob said and pat him on his curly head.

Junior sat down.

Jacob glanced at me and I swore I saw a few tears in his green eyes. I wanted the day to go well, and it was already so much better than I had anticipated.

"Now, it's your turn, Montana," he said, having already grabbed the silver slide that helped little ones to guide their ball.

"How I do it?" she asked, looking at the slide like she didn't know what to make of it.

"Here, I'll help you." He placed her ball on top of it.

She cautiously walked toward him, and he grabbed her hand and put it on the ball, when she was standing in position. With a slight push, he guided the ball down the slide and onto the lane.

Montana's eyes were big when she turned around and looked at me. She then looked back down at the pins and half of them fell down. She jumped up with enthusiasm she'd seen from her brother. "Mommy, Mommy," she yelled. "You see it?"

I chuckled, "I see it, sweetie."

She rolled it, again, knocking down two more, and she seemed every bit as pleased.

Then, it was my turn. I walked up to the lane and removed the tool that Montana used.

"Need some coaching?" Jacob asked with a wink. "I could stand behind you to guide it in."

I shook my head. "Down boy...just step back and watch how it's done," I bragged.

He glared at me. "Oh, I like a woman who knows how to trash talk."

I rolled my eyes, turned on my heels and rolled the ball. It went down the lane and knocked down all the pins. "I talk trash, but I can back it up," I quipped.

"Not bad," he muttered his surprise.

I shrugged, walked past him and gave Montana a high five. "Just a little girl power," I said, teasing him.

He picked up his ball and postured to roll his ball. He, too, got a strike. We locked eyes and he said, "I'm coming for you, girls."

"Bring it!" I looked at Montana and Junior. They were laughing just from seeing the pins fall. Our day couldn't have gotten off to a better start.

****

"We should do that again sometime," I said, putting Montana in a highchair and glancing at Jacob.

He rolled his eyes and looked at Junior. "You better get used to women bragging. They win one little game and that's all they want to talk about."

I laughed when Junior nodded his understanding. "Mommy, can't you just stop it?" he asked using Jacob's sarcastic tone.

"Okay, I'll drop it." I playfully glared at Jacob and then Junior. I giggled and took a swig of my soda.

Then Montana clapped her tiny hands together. "We win...we win!" she yelled.

"That's my girl," I said and gave her another high five. "I said, I'd drop it, but I can't make any guarantees about Montana."

"I had a lot of fun, even though me and Mr. Jacob didn't win," Junior spoke, after the waitress brought our lunch.

"I'm glad you enjoyed it," Jacob replied. "That makes us all winners then."

Junior seemed to be thinking and then he asked, "Don't you want your own kids?"

"Montie Jr.!" I scolded. "Why would you ask him that question?"

Jacob raised his hand to quiet me.

"No, it's a fair question. Junior, I love kids and would give anything to be blessed to have a couple, or three, one day. I just never was lucky enough to find the right woman to have my kids." Jacob hesitated looking in my direction, and when he did I saw how important having his own children was to him. "You'll understand one day, buddy," Jacob turned his attention back to Junior.

Junior nodded and grabbed a crayon. "Nah, I don't want any kids, ever," Junior replied and got lost in coloring a picture. "I just wanted to know if you wanted my mama to give you children and would that be my sister or brother?"

"When I do have children, I could only hope that it's with a woman as amazing as your mother, but me and your mother have not discussed having children because we're not ready for that yet," Jacob explained to Junior, who simply nodded and kept coloring.

"You are amazing, Jacob," I whispered.

"They make it easy," Jacob said, as he reached under the table and intertwined his fingers with mine. He moved closer to me and kissed my cheek.

The rest of our table conversation was easy, with Junior monopolizing most of the topics. Jacob was on every wavelength with my son, and I loved that. Jacob had his approval and mine.

Standing at my front door at the end of our family date, I unlocked the door, and Jacob stepped inside. The look in his eyes told me what he wanted.

"Hey, how about a movie?" I asked Montana and Junior, ushering them toward the living room. I held up my finger and left Jacob standing there, so that I could put a movie on for them. "Give me just a second."

"Yah!" they replied in unison as they followed behind me. It took a few minutes to pick out a movie, with Junior being the most opinionated about what it should be. Finally, they agreed upon Shrek.

"Okay, you guys watch this quietly until I come back in here, okay?"

"We will, mama," Junior said and sat on the sofa.

Montana sat beside him and started singing the intro song.

I went back out to the foyer and wrapped my arms around Jacob's neck. "I don't want you to go," I whispered huskily.

"I know, babe, and the last thing I want to do is leave here tonight. Do you see what just your hug has done to me?" I trailed his gaze down to the growing bulge in his slacks.

"Oh my."

"That's putting it mildly," he said as he adjusted his pants. "I don't want to confuse the kids and have them thinking more than they should right now," he admitted.

I loved the fact that he considered their feelings. I looked down at the floor thinking, but then felt his finger underneath my chin. "Chin up, beautiful. The next time the kids are with their father, I'll spend the night doing things to you that you've never had done before. I promise you that." His lips pressed against mine, and his tongue owned every corner of my mouth. I was his, as his hand slowly inched up my shirt—a sign of what we both wished could take place. After he had his feel, he removed his hand and slowly tugged away from our embrace. "I better go," he whispered.

"Yeah," I said, knowing exactly what heat level we were ascending to, if he kept seducing me. But I couldn't hide my disappointment, when he turned away from me and walked to his car, no matter how hard I tried.

CHAPTER FOURTEEN

JACOB

Going Back to Miami

I boarded my jet headed back to Miami. I had pressing business to handle, but for the entire flight I kept thinking about how much fun I had with Montie Jr. and Montana. I hadn't laughed that much in quite a long time. Then visions of the way Destiny smiled the other night when I carried her to her bedroom and put on her pajamas assailed my mind. Her pretty, brown face was so peaceful and happy. I could see her in my life forever. I couldn't wait until the day I could make things official between us. My hope was to keep her that happy for a very long time. I hated putting so many miles between us, but after receiving a call from Brian in accounting, I had to take this trip.

Brian informed me that the twenty-two million dollar bid we placed had been green-lighted by the Department of Defense. I had no doubt the DOD would award us the contract, and we would execute it with top-notch ability. My team of A1 vice presidents could handle it, but I was personally popping into the office to get the ball rolling. I always got my hands dirty when we had developments with over ten million in capital. These projects had to go off without a hitch.

So, I begrudgingly called Destiny to tell her I would be gone at least a week. She said she understood, but I could hear the disappointment in her voice. She wished me luck with the project, and to be frank, that's all I needed to hear. I planned to have a couple board meetings about the Delaware office's grand opening, too, while I was in Miami.

"Good morning, Mr. Turner," two of my staff members said as I walked through Turner Enterprises, reminding me how much I thrived off being in the center of the action. After all, Miami was where my family business began, and I was proud to be at the helm. I came from a long lineage of men who garnered the respect I was receiving. I stepped right into the shoes they left me and worked savagely hard to fill them.

"Good morning," I said to Jalisa Jeffers, my Vice President of Operations, when she approached me in the hallway that led to my office.

"Good morning, sir, and welcome back to Miami. Are we still on for the meeting at nine?"

"Yes, and bring the estimates for the DOD and a printed draft of this month's financials with you. Ask Tom to bring whatever figures you don't have available. He was working on them for me, too," I said. It used to drive them crazy to know that I had two

116

people working on the same task, but now they're used to me being thorough, and they know I expect the same from them.

"Yes sir. I'll see you in a few," Jalisa said as she walked toward her office.

"Howdy Wanda," I addressed my long-time secretary in the same way my father did during his tenure. Wanda wore a purple jacket with matching pants and shoes. Her hair was in a bun with a purple ribbon tied around it. My father hired her because she brightened up the place all those years ago, and at seventy she still remains vibrant and full of life.

"Why good morning, Mr. Turner! I left some notes for you on your desk. Since you were planning to come in today, I didn't email them to you. I hope that's okay."

Wanda was used to memos and sticky notes. I had gotten her into the digital world with emails, faxes, and even a little social media, and she complies with my request to be emailed, most of the time.

"That's perfectly fine, Wanda. Thanks." I unlocked my office and went in. The smell of fresh mahogany from my unique, handcrafted desk and bookcase impaled my senses. I flipped the light switch on and stared around the large room that had become my second home. I sat down in my Design Toscano chair behind my desk, and began going through the notes on my desk. One name stood out like a thorn: Justine.

She'd left three messages in the past thirty minutes on my office's voicemail, begging me to call her when I got into the office. When she called again, I buzzed Wanda's desk.

"Yes sir?"

"How did Justine know I would be here today?" I huffed out, allowing my frustration with my ex to be evident.

"Sir, she called and asked for you early this morning, and I told her you would be in later. You didn't tell me to screen her calls, so I hope that's okay."

I looked at my watch. It was only 8:30.

"What time did she call?"

"Eight a.m. on the dot." She paused. "Actually sir, she calls every morning at eight a.m. to see if you are here. Today was just the first day she called that you were scheduled to come in."

"Thanks, Wanda, but from now on I don't want you to give her any information as to when I'll be in the office. Just take a message and that's all." I hung up the phone and sighed. Not only had Justine been blowing up my cell, she was calling my office every morning.

At one point, I longed for our old friendship to be intact again, but she only wanted to talk about us getting back together as a couple. No matter how many times I told her it wasn't going to happen, she couldn't bring herself to believe me. What was it going to take to get it through her head that it was over?

I spent a few minutes answering messages. My nine o'clock meeting quickly approached, and by eleven my team had assembled a plan, handling every detail for the DOD's project down to the letter. I didn't even have to be here. That's how well they had written the plan. It felt good knowing I could count on them in my absence. I congratulated each of them on a job well done and exited the boardroom.

Justine approached me and frantically wrapped her arms around my waist. "Jacob!" she screamed, causing everyone to look at her. "Jacob, I've missed you so much. Please tell me you're not leaving town anytime soon."

I patted her back, as my VP team exited the board room behind me. "Hi Justine," I said, observing her as I drew back from her intrusive embrace.

I had to admit that she looked good with her nude makeup, flowing blonde curls, and eyes beautiful as the sky on a sunny day. She was toned and tight, and I didn't see one flaw in her appearance. And, to top it all off, she smelled delectably good.

"Jacob, we need to talk," she said, sounding somber.

"I'm kind of in the middle of something. Can I call you to talk about it later?" I spoke tight lipped.

"No, we can't talk about it later. This is urgent. I've been calling you for a month and you haven't answered. Who do you think I am? I don't like the way you're treating our relationship, and we need to talk about it, *now*," she said in a quivering voice that got more pitiful as she continued.

Wanda looked up from her computer with wide-eyed shock. A few other workers paid close attention to our exchange, showing sympathy for Justine, and that's when I knew I had to get her out of there.

"Come inside my office." I stepped inside my office and closed the door behind us with her following close behind. "Justine, you can't come into my business making a fool of yourself. You know we're not involved anymore, and I don't know what else to tell you other than the truth."

She grabbed my hand and held it close to her face. "Tell me that you're still in love with me the way I'm in love with you, Jacob."

"I can't do that," I said removing my hand from her face.

"Why? Why can't you, Jacob? Why can't you tell me that you love me? I know you haven't lost your feelings for me so soon after we broke up."

"Because...I—" I ran my hand over my beard and stared into her eyes—the same eyes I turned to for consolation at points in my life when I needed it most. "Justine, I do love you, and I always will. We're friends and have been the best of friends for years, so I will always love you that way."

"But you aren't in love with me?" she asked painfully.

"No, I'm not."

"It's her isn't it? That damned black—"

"Don't do it, Justine," I warned, and she paused mid-breath, as I dared her lips to move. "Yes, I'm in love with Destiny," I continued. "And, from the moment I fell in love with her, I've known for sure that I never was in love with you."

She toppled over in anguish as if she'd just been shot in the chest. Clasping her heart, she wept, "Jacob, I can't believe what you're saying to me. What are you saying?"

"I'm saying I'm sorry we ended the way we did, but I'll never be sorry for loving Destiny. She's the new woman in my life. I love her, and I want you to at least respect what we have."

"I will never respect that, and I don't understand how you expect me to! This is just going too far, Jacob. I stepped aside and allowed you time to go have your little jungle fever, but you can't be serious about this nigger," Justine said, peering into my eyes as if she were the one pissed. I thought I knew Justine well. She had never said anything disrespectful like that in all the years I'd known her.

I closed the space between us and grabbed her by the collar. "Didn't I tell you not to disrespect Destiny? When you called her a bitch, I overlooked it, because you were suicidal. But don't you ever again come out of your stupid ass mouth with anything like that about her ever in your miserable life. Since I've known you for so long, I'm going to give you another chance to get your head right," I spat fire and brimstone in Justine's face as I spoke, only pushing her away when I got my point across.

"Jacob, she *is* a nigger and a bitch. You need to get used to hearing the truth about people like her. I mean, you are a fucking billionaire and you want to run off to the hood and settle down with the first hood queen you find," she said nastily.

"That's it. Get the fuck out of here and don't ever come back, Justine." I grabbed her arm and pulled her toward the door. "It's just as well if we never see each other again," I added.

"This is not the end of this, Jacob," she said, holding her arm and grimacing in pain. "You will hear from me again."

"Oh, this is the end, Justine. I thought I knew you, but, with the way you're talking, we can't even be friends."

Her tone softened. "Jacob, we can get past this. We can fall in love again. All you have to do is forget about her and try to love me."

"Even if I believed that I could turn my feelings off and on like that, I don't want to get past what just happened here," I said, disappointed in the person standing before me. "I don't even associate with people that would say the things you said today. I don't want to ever see you again," I said, not believing that our friendship had come to ruins like this.

"Fine," she grated out through tight lips. "But it's not me who changed. It's you that I don't know," she tossed over her shoulder as she rushed out my door and through the reception area.

I plopped down in my chair, reached for the bottle of scotch I kept in my bottom drawer, and let out a deep sigh. I didn't bother getting a glass; I just drank it straight from the bottle.

"Sir, is everything okay?" Wanda peeked in to ask after Justine stormed past her desk.

"Everything's fine now that she is gone. Make sure security knows that she's not allowed on the property anymore," I said.

"Yes, sir," Wanda replied. She went to her desk, leaving me to make sense of the mess that had become of a lifelong friendship.

CHAPTER FIFTEEN

DESTINY

Sunday Surprise

That next Sunday, I got up and got ready for church. I wished the kids were home to go with me, but their dad had taken them since he had to cut his last weekend short. Jacob was in Miami handling business. He had been gone since Monday and we hadn't talked much. He had a lot to catch up with at his office. However, after the first full day passed without a call, my mind kept telling me he was with Justine.

I whipped into the crowded church parking lot, hoping a little spiritual cleansing would clear those negative thoughts from my mind. But, when I walked in and saw all of the couples together, I only thought about Jacob more. I shook the pastor's hand and entered the sanctuary. My eyes scanned the pews from the front to the back, looking for a good seat. My jaw dropped open and I gasped, when Jacob stood up from a seat in the back and waved at me.

"I definitely wasn't expecting to see you here. What are you doing here?" I asked when I reached him.

"Wait a minute. Is that how you greet me?"

"No, it's just that..." I paused. "You're here."

"Can't a guy attend church without being questioned?" Jacob joked.

"I guess so, but you're supposed to be in Miami," I prodded, while wrapping my mind around the surprise of seeing him.

He slipped his hand into mine. "No, I'm right where I'm supposed to be, Destiny."

"I'm glad you came," I smiled and took the seat beside him.

We read along with the scripture and sang along with the hymns. It felt like we were an actual family and the only thing missing was my two kids. Still, the thought of Jacob being with Justine when he was in Miami invaded my mind as the pastor began benediction.

"Want to go get a bite to eat?" Jacob asked, when service was over.

"Yeah, I would like that."

"Great, we can take my car and I'll bring you back to get yours when we're done."

"That's fine with me."

We rode to the restaurant in comfortable silence. He pulled into the parking lot of Tazi's and I glanced at the smile on his face. "I figure this is as good a place as any to go. Ever been?" he asked, shooting me a teasing grin.

"Once or twice."

"Would you like to share a chocolate dessert with me?"

"I would love that."

He opened my door and we headed into the restaurant. He got us a table and we took our seats. We had been there enough that neither one of us needed to look in a menu when we placed our orders. I glanced around the restaurant, taking in the familiar scenery before turning back to face him. His eyes focused on me.

"Seeing you at church today was a shocker. I don't believe this is real, right now."

"I told you I'm wherever you are, so if you're at church, I'm at church. I'm all in, and this is just another step in that direction," he said confidently.

"Bringing me to Tazi's, is that also to show me that you're all in?" I asked, remembering our first encounter with a devilish grin splayed across my face.

"Well...that and the fact that someone hooked me on the three-layer chocolate mousse cake. From that day forward, I will never look at chocolate the same," he teased, biting down on his bottom lip.

"Hmm..." I said, tapping my finger on the table. "Is this someone I know?"

"Just some woman I met who introduced me to two dripping with sweetness, mouth-watering chocolate desserts in one day."

"Well, she must some kind of woman, Jacob. You should snatch her up and never let her go," I replied.

"Oh, she's scrumptious, and you bet I'm not letting her go. I'm following her around like a stray pup now," he opened his mouth and started panting.

We shared so many laughs before our food came out. We ate without missing a beat in our conversation. After we had eaten delicious deli sandwiches, pickles and chips, we ordered chocolate mousse cake for old time's sake. Jacob paid for our meals and we headed back to the church to get my car. Our conversation in the car was light, until his phone rang.

"It's Justine," he said, after looking at his caller ID. "She's been calling me nonstop since I saw her in Miami." He looked at me as if he wanted me to advise him on how to handle her, and I was about to chime in until I recalled what he said.

"Wait a minute. You saw her when you were in Miami this week?"

"She came to my office and I told her it was over, but she's insistent that we can work things out. When I told her that the only woman I want is you, she went off the deep end," he confided.

"How did she know you were going to be in Miami?" I asked, wondering if Jacob was even telling the whole truth.

"My secretary told her."

"Did you check your secretary about that?" I fumed.

Justine's persistence to be in the picture made me feel some type of way. They had a history I could never make up with him, and I knew the depths that a woman would go through to get a man. This had to be nipped in the bud before it spiraled out of control.

"Yes, I have everything handled with her. I don't want you to worry about her, Destiny. After what I told her, she should have the picture."

"Why is she still calling you though, Jacob?" I sounded more pissed than I wanted to sound. "I'm not trying to sound rude. I just want to know what's going on with her," I rephrased.

"I haven't been answering to find out."

"Well, until she stops calling, she's going to be a problem. I know women who have been scorned and some of them are still pining over the men that left them behind."

"See that's the thing. I don't want to leave her behind entirely. I wish we could have our old friendship back, but she wants more."

"Of course she does, Jacob. Most women don't cross the line and jump back over it on a whim. She's probably dangerously in love with you," I said, and thought about the implications of a mentally unstable woman grieving over the man I was involved with.

"I wish we never crossed that line," Jacob said as he parked his car beside mine. "I might have to change my number."

"That might be the best thing to do. Because even if she's listening to your voice message or just hoping that you'll pick up may be giving her unjust hope that she'll get through to you."

"Then it's settled. I'll have Wanda get me a new number set up tomorrow," Jacob said before he got out and rushed around to open the door for me.

"Thanks for lunch, Jacob," I spoke, feeling a pit in my stomach as I exited his car. "But Jacob, I'm not going to deal with any more mess with Justine. If you ever choose to stand by her side over mine again, we're done."

"Destiny, wait. Don't walk away from me!" I heard him call after me, but I stormed toward my car. I searched for my keys but couldn't find them fast enough to get in before he reached me. He ran a finger under my jaw and I turned to face him. We remained in that position, eyes interlocked.

"What do you want to say, Jacob?"

"When we go out and have fun like we just did...it's just so perfect. I don't want you to leave upset with me. In my heart, I'm doing the right thing by you. I've told

Justine that I don't want to see her again and to leave me alone."

"Jacob, all of that is good. But before I met you, I was an independent woman, and didn't feel like I needed anyone. I won't let my feelings hold me hostage in this relationship, either, just because Justine is playing games, and she is. I know a woman's games when I see them." I swallowed the lump in my throat, pulled away from him and got into my car.

"Destiny..." I heard his voice fade out as I drove away.

I didn't want to lose him. However, the thought of him kissing Justine like he did the night I saw him at Lapidus reeled me back in from the fantasy world I'd been living in. I had to give some genuine thought to our future...for my kids and myself. I refused to get so far out in his ocean where I couldn't reach the shore and ended up drowning in his love.

CHAPTER SIXTEEN

DESTINY

I Think I Love You, Again

I was finishing vacuuming when I heard the front door open. "Hello, we're here," Montie Sr. called from the foyer. I was excited to have my kids back in the house, and had left the door unlocked for their arrival.

"Hello, hello," I called out, entering the foyer as well.

Junior and Montana ran to me.

"Mama, mama!" they both yelled excitedly.

"I've missed you both so much!"

Junior pulled away and looked up at me. "It's only been a couple days."

"Oh, you're Mr. Big Guy today. You don't miss mama?" I asked with fake sadness.

"Yes, I do, mama," he said.

"I know you've only been gone a few days, but I always miss you when you're gone." I rubbed his curly head of hair and roughed him up a little.

Montana's eyes searched around the foyer.

"Lose something?" I asked, teasingly.

"Where's Acob?"

I nearly fell over. I expected it from Junior, but Montana didn't seem as aware of our connection.

"He's home," I responded casually. "Why don't you both say goodbye to your dad and we'll talk about it later."

They ran back over and hugged Montie's legs. I heard their tiny muffled voices say, "Goodbye, Daddy,"

"Goodbye, see you both soon," Montie answered.

The kids left the foyer, and I turned to him. "Did you guys have a good weekend?" I asked.

"We did," he nonchalantly spoke, and then cocked his head. "I know I have no business asking this, but is everything okay with you and this Jacob cat?"

"You're right; you have no business asking this." I walked to the door and opened it for him.

He didn't move, but instead kept watching me. "Seems a bit odd that you're here alone; after all, since you started dating dude I don't recall ever seeing you alone, and the kids say he's always here."

"First of all, that's not true. Secondly, again, it's none of your business. Now, if you would please leave."

"You don't need to get so defensive. I'm only trying to point out that it's unusual to find you here alone. If he was out of town or busy with work then that's one thing, but if you two separated, I believe that I have a right to know."

I placed my hands on my hips. "Why would you have the right to know? What Jacob and I do is our business!

You don't get the right to know everything about me. You lost that right the day we got a divorce."

"I do believe I struck a nerve," he said.

I couldn't be sure, but for a moment, I thought he was smiling about that fact.

I looked away from him. "Montie, I don't have time for your drama."

"Destiny, I have the right to know who is and isn't going to be in my children's lives. It affects my parenting."

"How?"

"It just does."

"Let me just put it this way. Jacob may not be here, but we are fine," I concluded our back and forth.

"Are you sure?"

"Ugh..." I groaned. "Just go! It's not your concern and I don't have any intention of talking about it with you."

"Fine." He moved to the door, but turned back around before leaving. "For the record, if he did something stupid then I stand by your leaving him." He winked at me and I stared at him in disbelief. "In case you were wondering."

He walked out the door.

I slammed it shut behind him.

"Unbelievable," I mumbled along with other blasphemous sentiments.

Moving away from the foyer, I went into the living room. I just wanted to focus on Junior and Montana and forget about everything else.

****

For the next week, Jacob was back in Atlanta but completely absorbed with the opening of the Delaware office. When he wasn't having phone meetings, I was meeting my clients during the evening or doing extracurricular activities with my children. It wasn't easy not being able to talk to him when I wanted to. At times, I would see something that Junior or Montana was doing and knew Jacob would appreciate it. I would instantly run to the phone to call him, but then back away, because he told me his schedule would be hectic.

As the week wound down from work, I thought about what to do for the weekend. I walked into the living room where I spotted the kids each coloring a picture. I smiled at them, both oblivious to the fact that I was watching. It had been awhile since the three of us had done anything by ourselves, and it was a beautiful day outside.

"What do you say we go to the park?" I asked, waiting for them to look up.

"Just the three of us?" Junior asked.

"That's the general idea," I answered with a smile.

He frowned, and I fought the urge to ask why he looked upset. Once he began talking, I didn't need to wonder.

"It's been awhile since I saw Jacob. Does he want to see us anymore?" he asked.

Pain shot through my heart.

Junior had confused Jacob's absence with rejection. He shouldn't feel the need to carry the burden of anything happening in my and Jacob's relationship.

"Oh, honey," I began, and sat down on the couch. I patted the two spots next to me "I need to talk to you both."

Montana pulled herself up. I didn't think she would quite understand, but she did ask about him, too.

"Jacob adores you both very much, almost as much as I love you. It is killing him that he can't hang out with you guys. He has a lot going on at his job, and he has to take care of that first. I promise you the minute he can, he'll come back here and we'll all go out again. Okay?"

Junior seemed to think on it, and finally nodded his understanding.

Montana stared at the floor. "I miss Acob," she finally said.

I pulled them both close to me.

"I miss Acob, too," I said.

It meant a lot to me that she felt that way and that Junior wanted him around. I made the right decision about having him in our lives.

"Go to the bathroom and get washed up. I'll be there in a second to help you," I said, and they rushed off.

I stared after them, both such blessings in my life.

I was just getting up when I heard the doorbell. I peeked through the peephole and saw Montie Sr. outside. I opened the door and shook my head.

"What are you doing here?"

"That's a fine welcome," he laughed, entering the house without an invitation.

"Don't you have some work to do, or something? Anything besides showing up here? Is something wrong?" I asked.

"Nothing's wrong. I just thought I would swing by and see the kids."

It definitely was not like him to come by on his off weekend. "Well, you kind of picked the wrong time to make an unexpected visit. We're going out."

"Oh? Where to?" He asked, glancing around the house.

"It's not any of your business where I'm going, but, if you must be nosey, we're going to the park," I blurted out and rolled my eyes to the heavens.

"It's been ages since I've been to a park. Is Jacob going?"

"No, just me and the kids."

"Care if I tag along?"

"Yes, I do care," I snapped. "This is time for just the three of us. I don't interfere with your plans and I would appreciate you not interfering with mine."

I quickly glanced down the hall to make sure the kids weren't listening.

"Now..." I lowered my voice, "If you don't mind, I would appreciate it if you would leave. I would like to get on with *my* weekend."

Montie stood firm...unwavering.

Junior came out of the bathroom. His eyes focused on Montie Sr. and grew in size. "Daddy!" he called, running and crashing into Montie.

"Hey, buddy." Montie smiled at me and kissed our son on the forehead.

"Junior, where's your sister?" I asked.

"She's waiting for you in the bathroom," he said and turned back to Montie. "Are you coming with us to the park?"

My heart fell the minute I heard him ask the question.

"Junior, he is too busy today," I said, glaring at Montie.

"Oh..." Junior's lips went into pouting formation.

"I'm never too busy for you, son," Montie said, pulling him into a hug. "I'd love to go to the park with you guys. That's if it's okay with your mother."

My jaw dropped, and I stormed down the hall to go help Montana. Montie was weaseling his way into my plans with the kids and I couldn't do anything about it without looking like an ass.

Thirty minutes later, I pushed Montana while Montie Sr. pushed Junior on the swings. Everyone seemed to be having a great time, but I was wondering why Montie Sr. was even there. Periodically, he glanced at me and winked or smiled, which caught me off guard. This wasn't the way my day was supposed to go.

After the swings, the kids wanted to go down the slide again. I hung back, letting them play and kicked myself for getting caught up on this faux family day.

"Thank you so much for inviting me," Montie said.

I glared at him. "I didn't...our son did."

He shrugged, "You didn't do anything to stop it, so I figured you must have been okay with it."

"What could I say, Montie? I wasn't going to let Junior down, even though the last thing I wanted was for you to come along. I wanted some time alone with the kids...something you always get and I never get."

"That's by your own choice," he shot back. "You have them far more time than I do, but you bring Jacob into the picture and choose to allow him to tag along with you and the kids wherever you go."

Montie was punishing me for trying to be happy and that bothered me. "The point is, I don't understand why you're here," I hissed between my teeth.

He looked away, watching Montana as she slid down the slide. She was laughing and then it was Junior's time. Montie was engrossed in watching the kids play, and I wondered if he forgot what I said. Finally, he turned to me.

"You want to know why I came over today?" he asked.

"I said I did," I sarcastically replied.

He was more nervous than I had ever seen him before. His chocolate dimples formed in his otherwise smooth face as he said, "I'm worried about you."

"Worried about me? That's odd. Why would you be worried about me now, when you weren't worried about me when I was your wife?"

He fidgeted from one foot to another. "You seemed happy with your new boyfriend and then all of sudden he's not around. I came over to check things out."

I laughed. "So you wanted to spy on me?"

"Yeah, I wanted to see if Jacob was there. If he was, then I could move on and forget about it, but if he weren't...then I would need to be worry about your well-being. I want you to be happy."

"Montie, you don't have to be concerned," I replied, averting my attention from his solemn eyes. "Jacob and I are fine. He's busy working. We're not breaking up, but there comes a time when two people need a breather to handle their own business, you know?"

"Humph. Tell me about it," he spoke.

It bothered me the way he said that, seeming to lump Jacob and me into the same category as our dead marriage. "You have no clue what I mean," I replied.

"You and I needed a breather and we took one." He stepped closer to me so that our faces were a few inches apart. "Now may be the time to get back together."

My eyes followed Junior and Montana, who were racing each other to the merry-go-round. I watched them get on as another adult was pushing it around for her son.

"Montie, you and I aren't taking a breather. We finalized a divorce, for crying out loud! And that's because there were things more important to you in life than our marriage. Now, I'm with Jacob, who loves me and I love him. We'll work through whatever comes our way." My eyes tore away from the merry-go-round to look at him. "I don't want you interfering with our relationship."

He grabbed my hand. "Destiny, I can't let you go without telling you that I'm still deeply in love with you."

"You're not in love with me, Montie," I argued, removing my hand from his. "You just don't want to see me happy with someone else."

He stood up and reached for my hand again. "Destiny, listen..."

"Montie, stop that. Don't touch me."

"Destiny, in my heart, I owe it to myself and to you to be truthful. I seriously am still in love with you. I never for one minute stopped being in love with you."

"You think you're still in love with me? Maybe you are in love with the idea of me. I *am* the mother of your children. I stood by you, work and all, until our marriage was over and I had nothing left to give you. I just can't..." my words trailed off at the sound of a shrilling scream. Montana was lying on the ground hollering in agony. I rushed to her side.

"I...I am so sorry," the woman was muttering. Tears started falling down the stranger's face. "I didn't see that she was starting to fall off."

"I'm sure she'll be fine," I said to console the woman.

"Mommy..." Montana cried out. As she attempted to sit up, an angry gash along her chin bled out. I immediately knew she would need stitches.

I glanced at Montie, our conversation out of my mind, and he picked Montana up.

"Let's get to the hospital," he said as I grabbed Junior's hand.

CHAPTER SEVENTEEN

DESTINY

By My Side

I sat in the waiting room, wringing my hands together, on edge about Montana being with the doctor. It was only stitches, but she was still young and I wanted to be there for her. The staff kept insisting that she would be fine in the back without me.

"Destiny, I'm sorry we weren't paying attention to them, but she could've had the accident either way," Montie reasoned.

I glared at him. "That's not the point. We should've never been in this situation to start with. We're divorced, and as far as I am concerned, nothing has changed. If I weren't distracted by you today, I would have been by her side the entire time."

My phone rang, and I glanced at the caller ID. Jacob's number lit up, as if he had intuition enough to know that I needed to hear from him at that very moment.

"I'll be back," I mumbled and glanced at Junior, "Do you mind watching him?"

"He's my son; of course not," Montie said with an incredulous look on his face.

"Good." I got up and headed around the corner. "Hello?" I answered the phone, my voice crackling as if I were going cry at any moment.

"Destiny?" Jacob said my name, and a whirlwind of emotions swept up inside of me causing me to sob. "Baby, what's wrong? Talk to me," Jacob insisted.

"I just glad to hear from you," I said above a sniffle. "You won't believe the horrible day I've had. Montie came over, and we all went to the park, and then..."

"Wait a minute. Montie went with you to the park?" he asked, cutting into my rambling.

"Yes. The kids wanted him to, but that's not the worst part. We were arguing and I lost track of Montana until she screamed after falling off the merry-go-round. She has a big cut on her face, and we're at the emergency room now. She has to get stitches. It's a nice-sized cut, so I hope her face heals. God, I hope it's not permanent." I controlled my erratic breaths as I continued. "Sorry, I sound like a blubbering idiot. I wasn't expecting you to call. What were you calling for?"

There was a long hesitation on the other end. "I just had an inkling that I needed to see how you were doing. Now, I know why. I want to be there for you, Destiny, but I'm sure Montie is there and I don't want to get in the way of your family. But all you have to do is tell me you want me to come to the hospital."

"Do what you feel is right, Jacob."

"What do you mean by that?"

"I mean, I just told you what happened. I shouldn't have to tell you what to do next."

"You don't have to, baby. I'm on my way." He ended the call.

I went back to the waiting room and sat down, feeling better already.

The doctor came out of the room and I quickly stood up. "Thanks for being patient with us. It's sometimes easier to do these procedures when parents aren't in the room, and especially in Montana's case where she wanted you to hold her. She was calmer once you left out. At any rate, she has twelve stitches. It was a deep cut; however, I'm confident scarring will be minimal."

"Thank you so much for taking good care of our daughter," I said, breathing a sigh of relief as I glanced at Montie.

"Accidents like this happen all the time, and it's our pleasure to be able to help. You may go in and sit with Montana, while the nurse gets your discharge instructions on how to care for the stitches ready," the doctor said before he went back through the same door from which he had come.

Montie Sr. gawked and asked, "Why's he here?"

My attention went to the entrance and I smiled when I saw Jacob walking toward us. "I asked him to come. Thank you so much for coming right away, Jacob. I was just getting ready to go back to check on Montana. The doctor says we can be with her now."

"Of course, I'm here, babe," Jacob said.

"Jacob!" Junior ran to him and threw his arms around Jacob.

I couldn't help but look at Montie who let out a loud huff. Irritation rippled through his eyes as he stood there fuming.

"Let's go check on Montana," Jacob said.

I wanted Jacob by my side, but Montie wasn't going for it. "They only allow two people back at a time," said Montie.

"Oh, no problem. I'll wait out here with Junior, while you two go back," Jacob said, understanding. I gave him a gracious look, as Montie and I headed through the double doors to Montana's room.

She jumped up and down when we entered. "Mommy...Daddy...I hungry."

I laughed, thankful to see that she was fine. "We'll get you something to eat as soon as you get out of here. The doctor said you got your stitches like a big girl. Let me see them," I lifted her chin.

"I did it like a big girl, like you told me to, mama."

I hugged her neck and said, "Good job, sweetie. Hey, you know who's in the waiting room and wanting to see you?"

She shook her head. "No."

"Jacob..."

Her eyes got big. "Acob here?"

"How about you let me hold my own daughter, before you go throwing his name around?" Montie said sarcastically.

"You're too much," I said underneath my breath and rolled my eyes at Montie. I leaned down and kissed Montana's forehead. "I'll go get Jacob and let him come in for a few minutes."

Before I left out the room, I heard Montie say, "Montana, I'm sorry that you fell and hurt yourself, but I'm glad you're better. Daddy loves you."

"I wub you, Daddy."

When I walked back into the room with Jacob and Junior, Montie hugged Montana. Her eyes lit up when Montie stepped away and she could see Jacob.

"Acob!"

"That's some bandage you have there," he said, leaning over the bed and hugging her. "Did it hurt?"

"Not weally," she spoke.

"As soon as the doctor lets you go, we'll grab a bite to eat," I interrupted. I smiled, seeing how relaxed everyone was, until I looked at Montie.

"Yay!" the kids said in unison.

I laughed.

"I'll see you guys next weekend," Montie said and waved as he walked out the door.

"You're not going to eat with us?" I asked, catching up to him in the hallway.

He smirked. "Nah, I don't really have an appetite to sit anywhere chumming it up with you, the kids, *and* Jacob. That's a little overcrowded, don't you think?"

"Suit yourself." I shrugged. "I was only trying to be polite."

"Yeah, keep telling yourself that."

"What's your issue, Montie?"

"Just enjoy your dinner, Destiny."

CHAPTER EIGHTEEN

DESTINY

No Boundaries

Over the next few months, Jacob spent every chance he could with the kids and me, buying gifts and taking us places I never dreamed of going, like an impromptu midday trip to San Antonio just to ride the river boats. We were back in Atlanta before nightfall that day and I enjoyed every minute of it. The kids were comfortable around him, which made me feel good about opening up to him.

As much as I wanted to be in Jacob's my arms and share my nights with him, we made a pledge not to move in together until we were married. I didn't like when my kids went to their father's house, but I was excited for quality time with Jacob.

Friday rolled around, and the doorbell rang all too soon. The kids were busy watching cartoons, as I went to the door to greet my ex. He wore a smug smile, when I welcomed him inside.

"The kids are ready and—" I began. He put up his hand to stop me.

"Before I grab them and leave, can we talk?"

I wasn't interested in another conversation that he'd been bombarding me with every time his weekend came around. I turned on my heels and headed into the kitchen and took a seat at the table.

"What's up now?" I asked, nonchalantly.

"I want to discuss your boyfriend."

"You should be bored with asking questions about Jacob. Nothing that you have to ask has changed since the last time you asked. It seems like you would have found another topic by now, Montie." I crossed my arms.

"I'm concerned by the amount of time he spends around our children. We both know that he's a rich cat from Miami, but how much do you really know about his past?" Montie asked.

"One minute you're asking why he's not here. Now, you're saying he's here too much and questioning his character. I know more about Jacob than I knew about him, so don't worry about me, Montie. I know everything that I need to know. Is that all you wanted to ask?" I stood up.

"Don't get testy, Destiny. I have a right to ask as many questions as I need to feel comfortable about a man that you have in here over my children."

My mouth flew open to spew some not so very nice things, but I couldn't even get the first word out before he self-destructed.

"You've got this...white man spending time with my kids. Just because he's rich doesn't exempt him from being some kind of low life. And, the worst part of it is that he has my kids thinking he's their father. He's overstepping his boundaries, because Montie Jr. and Montana have a father that's here for them already?"

I nodded, finally understanding that his frustrations had nothing to do with Jacob's color or bank account. It didn't even have anything to do with jealousy.

"Montie, you're acting insecure. Your children will always know who their father is and that he loves them. I will make sure of it."

"What?" he spat, shaking his head. "I am not insecure. I have no doubt that Montie and Montana will always know I'm their father. I just don't like the idea of another person entering into the picture. It complicates things."

"Montie, there is no reason for you to worry about Jacob. He's a good man that has our children's best interest at heart, and no, he's not trying to take your place," I assured him.

"I just don't want them to get attached and, when he bores of you and suddenly decides to leave, they will be hurt."

"Get out of my house," I ordered through clenched teeth.

"What? I'm just speaking the truth."

"No, you're being messy. I don't know what is causing you to be concerned with what's happening in this house, when you weren't concerned with it when it was your home. But let me just be clear, I love Jacob, he loves me, and we are far from bored."

His eyes got big as he leaned back in the chair.

He crossed his arms and glared at me with disdain. "So, just like that, you love this motherfucker?"

"Montie, Montana, your dad's here. Get your bag and come on, sweeties," I called out and went to wait by the door. I heard their footsteps tracking toward where we were in the foyer.

"I am just concerned," Montie whispered close to my ear.

I leaned away from him and asked, "Now, who's overstepping boundaries?"

"Daddy," Montana said, breaking into the awkward moment. He swooped her up into his arms and hugged her while stealing glances at me.

Junior came into the foyer, as well. "Hey dad," he said.

"Are you ready to have some fun with your dad this weekend?" Montie asked them both.

"Yah!" said Montana.

"What are we going to do?" Junior asked.

"Well, I thought we could go see that new Transformers movie."

"Jacob already took us to see that," Junior said.

"Well, how about we see the Justice League? I got my hands on an advanced copy."

"Saw that one too," Junior said.

Montie looked at me, and I shrugged. If he wanted to be a good father to his kids, he had to step his game up, because Jacob was bringing it in a major way. I leaned down and kissed my babies, and waved as they left the house.

"Have a good time," I said.

****

Jacob arrived an hour later and I was still reeling over the indecency of Montie's concerns. When I opened the door, I was relieved to see him. I pulled him into the house and wrapped my arms around him, kissing his hot lips.

"God, I needed that," I moaned, smiling up at him. "You have no idea how much."

"Me too," he replied. "You know we could forfeit dinner and go straight for dessert," he winked at me, moving in for another kiss.

"As much as that sounds appetizing, I have been looking forward to getting out of the house for some adult interaction. How about we make it short and sweet?"

He groaned but nodded. "I guess I'll have to hang in there. You hear that man?" he said gesturing to the hard steel beneath his slacks.

"I know, it's a terrible life," I laughed. "Let me grab my purse."

When I got back to the door, he brushed his tongue against my lips. "This better be short, or else I'm going to punish you when we get back," he spoke raggedly.

"Well, what's a girl to do with that type of threat?" I bit down on my lip and reveled in his challenge. "Who knows, I might just take my punishment." I winked.

"Keep looking at me like that and I bet you won't make it to the damn car." He opened the door and pulled me to him and our bodies melded as one. His hands snaked down my back and palmed an ass full of cheeks. He pulled me closer to him, as if it were even possible. "I can't wait to make love to you," he muttered into the fold of my neck, where he left a trail of butterfly kisses.

After spinning my world out of control, he took my hand and escorted me to the car. Well, I floated behind him like an intoxicated sailor.

On the road to the restaurant, I found myself watching him. I loved him and I didn't care who knew it. The fact that my ex got me so riled up about it bothered me, but I was glad Montie knew that I was in love with Jacob.

"I love you, you know that, right?" I asked him.

"Yes, and you know how much I do love you."

I nodded and gazed out the window. No other words needed saying. I reached over and grabbed his hand.

We held hands the rest of the way to the restaurant. When we arrived, we went inside and they immediately sat us. It was my first time at Bacchanalia's. Therefore, Jacob placed our orders.

"I love the way you decorated my bedroom. You captured exactly what I wanted," he said making a note of the vintage American soldier pictures I framed to match his bedroom set. I found a commemorative US flag quilt for his bed to match.

"I'm glad you like it. It's been a while since you told me you wanted those pictures, so I knew you would be surprised when I went over today while you were in your meeting to put them up," I said, enjoying the glee in his eyes.

"I really was surprised, especially with the picture of my great grandfather in his uniform. That one got to me," Jacob said, staring at me for a long time. "I'm a lucky man to have found someone like you. I don't ever intend to let you go, not for any reason. I want you to be mine, forever."

"Whoa, I think I'm the lucky one. I'm just honored to be able to get something as memorable as those pictures done for you. You work hard and you deserve special things. It made me happy to do it," I replied, taking a drink of water. I had to take in the fact that Jacob just admitted to wanting me forever...like every day for the rest of his life. He'd told me before how he felt, but I believed what he'd just said like I believed in air to breathe. "How's the opening of the Delaware office going?" I asked, changing the subject.

"It's coming along; should be happening by the end of the month," he smiled, showing his pretty whites through his gorgeous beard.

"That's great news. Is everything still good with you working out of Atlanta? I mean, I know they miss you at the Miami headquarters," I fished for his feelings about the move.

"With me being here, we've had a spike in Georgia business and Miami is still strong, so it's a win-win financially."

"Why do I hear a but in your answer?"

"Sales increases are wonderful, but the downside is that headquarters is in Miami, so I'll be doing a lot of travel. I just want you to be aware of that, but I have no intention of leaving Atlanta, unless you and the kids are with me." His intense glare sent butterflies moving through my stomach.

"I'm fine with travel, as long as I know you're coming back."

"You'll never have to worry about that...ever." A sexy but dangerous look entered his eyes. "Why are you questioning whether I'm staying in Atlanta? Did Montie get out of line today when he picked up the kids?" he asked.

"I don't really want to talk about him." The waiter brought our food, while Jacob was giving me a concerned look. I took a bite of my salad.

"Don't play me for a fool, Destiny," he spoke, a hint of a smirk on his lips. "I can tell something is bothering you, and you're always like this when Montie's weekend rolls around."

I focused on my food, not making eye contact. His eyes burned a hole through me, so I couldn't look away for too long. "He's just Montie being Montie. No big deal," I said.

"See that's the kind of thing I'm not going to have happening with my woman. He's not going to keep coming around upsetting you like this and leaving me to have to deal with it. I think it's time for me and Montie to have a talk. Tell me what happened."

"Fine," I mumbled as I put my fork down. "Montie did say a few things today that got me thinking, that's all."

"Go on," Jacob sat back in his seat.

I swallowed the hard lump in my throat. "You wouldn't leave me because you were bored with me, would you?" I asked. "I try not to let him get to me, but I can't help but see the glaring similarity of his claim of what you'll do to me and what you did to Justine," there I said it. World War III was probably looming after my admission, but Jacob did leave Justine without warning after he hooked up with me in a bout of insta-love.

"So, you don't trust that what we have is real?"

"I'm not saying that, because I believe it is, but—"

"Look, Montie knows how to stir up your insecurities the same way Justine plays on my emotions. We can't let them do that to us. In order for us to work, we have to trust that if one of us walked off the side of the earth that it'll be okay to follow because that's how well we know each other's heart and intentions."

"I trust you, Jacob. I really do," I said.

"And I'm satisfied right where I am and I'm not leaving, even if Montie cries foul every two weeks," he said, looking intently at me. "Besides, your multiple personalities keep the excitement going."

I laughed, feeling a blush creeping up my neck.

"One minute he's asking why you aren't there. The next minute he's saying you're around too much and questioning your boundaries with the kids and..." I paused and took a sip of my wine.

"And what?"

"Talking about you being white."

"Does that bother you?" he asked, pushing his plate away from him.

"Not one bit. I wouldn't have you anyway but the way you are."

"Have the kids said anything about it?"

160

"No, they don't see color. They only see the love you show them."

"I don't care what anyone thinks as long as we all see the human side of each other. Everything else is other people's problems," he said and pulled his dinner plate back in front of him.

I picked up my fork and went back to enjoying dinner, as well. I didn't notice him glaring at me until I saw his fork still on the plate and he wasn't moving.

"Why aren't you eating?" I asked.

"Do you question my boundaries with your children?" he asked as his phone beeped. He glanced at it and looked annoyed. "I only want them to be comfortable around me, but if you think I need to back off..." he was saying.

"No! I love the way things are going. I wouldn't change it for anything." I gave him a reassuring smile. "Trust me...I believe we are moving in the right direction. I don't want you to change a thing."

"Good, because I have really been enjoying myself." Slowly, a smile crept on his lips and he finally started eating again.

"Me too. I'll tell you what, Jacob. Let's eat and go back to your condo to read a good book in your new bed. It looks sturdy enough for a lot of reading, but I wonder how sturdy it really is," I said.

"I'm sure it's sturdy enough for me to *read* you until you forget your ex's bullshit," he said.

I took a few more bites then looked at him. Suddenly, I was not nearly as hungry for food, but I had a thirst for knowledge that could only be found in the book of Jacob.

"What ex?" I giggled.

He laughed, put down the cash to pay for the bill, and grabbed my hand.

In no time, we were in the car, heading toward his place.

CHAPTER NINETEEN

JACOB

Satisfaction

I felt her lips on my neck as we crashed down to the bed. Her body was softly grinding underneath mine. "Oh God, you are so damn sexy, Destiny. Give me what's mine," I whispered against her heated, caramel colored skin, as I trailed my lips up to hers. My tongue dove deep inside of her mouth, excavating what I needed as our tongues eagerly sought one another out. As we kissed, I spread her legs and draped each over my shoulders. I reached my hand down to touch her ripened clit and groaned with desire. Guiding my rock hard cock into her warmth, I slipped inside her and our bodies just molded together.

"Oh Jacob," she whimpered as her soft body trembled against mine. She moaned repeatedly, as I thrusted deeper and deeper inside of her heat.

She clenched her thighs together and grinded her pelvis hard against mine, eagerly engulfing my full length. She pulled and I pushed. My enlarging steel pulsating with each thrust, she continued to milk me for all I was worth.

"That's right, fuck me baby!" I growled out. I didn't know how long I would last with the way she devoured me into her slippery tightness then released me only to accept me into her sweet heat once more. I traveled as deep into her body as I could fit.

"Oh. My. Dear. Heavens..." she cried out to the heavens as a violent wave rippled through her trembling body. "I'm coming, Jacob.

"Let it go, baby. How does it feel?" I stretched her legs wide and pounded inside of her, showing no mercy as her succulent cream coated my cock. "Say it. Tell me how it feels. Talk to me."

"Yes...yes...oh God yes, it feels so good! I can't take it anymore," she hollered and moaned, arching her back to receive each thrust with precision.

My poster bed banged against the wall. I didn't hear squeaking springs, which told me the bed was worth every penny. "Well, at least we know the bed is good," I said.

"Shut up and fuck...me," she screamed, as more of her juices sprang forth, covering my stomach and upper thighs.

I stroked her juicy cunt, making good on my promise that her ex-husband would be the last thing on her mind tonight. The only thing I wanted on her mind was the sensation that accompanied each stroke. The way her body constantly quivered beneath mine told me I accomplished that goal.

"I want to ride you," she muttered.

I rolled us over, allowing Destiny to take the reign. She slid down my cock with ease and, when she crashed onto me, I called out her name. "Destiny... Ugh... You're going to make me come," I breathed against her scorching hot skin, as my lips covered every reachable part of her body.

"Come with me, Jacob," she bounced unrelentingly atop of me.

I growled when a gush of cum ejaculated hard into her tight walls. Her legs trembled vigorously, causing her to collapse on top of me. I slowly released the grip I had on her hips and rolled on top of her. My lips explored her nipples, sucking them hard into my mouth then gently kissing them. Next, I had a focused takeover of her lips.

"Hmmm..." she moaned, slipping her tongue inside and seductively maneuvering it around my lips. She held tight around my neck. My arms wrapped snugly around her waist.

I flipped her over and lowered my body onto hers so that my chest pressed hard against her breasts. My tongue circled her earlobes as she whimpered beneath me. Trailing down to her neck, I sucked tenderly, nibbling lightly on her skin.

Our lovemaking became less of a conquest and more of a supernatural connection, as we remained eye to eye, in the heat of the moment. That's why we had to be forever. I could never go back to life without passion like this; there is no life without my Destiny.

"Ooooh Jacob—" she closed her eyes and whimpered again, this time digging her nails into my back. She looked so beautiful as I crawled up her body.

My erection grew thick between her thighs, and my breathing ragged. I slipped inside her heat and we made love until orgasm erupted through the both of us. I breathed pleasure heavily in her ear. The rhythm of our breaths lulled me to sleep, completely satisfied.

CHAPTER TWENTY

JUSTINE

One Last Chance

"Argh!" I screamed, when his voicemail picked up. I could not believe Jacob had dismissed me like a piece of worn out trash, after all the years I loved him unconditionally. I loved him when he was a big glasses wearing goofball that no one wanted to talk to. I remember the first time I took up for him, when the other kids were bullying him. I made them all back down.

"Jacob is my friend!" I told Rochelle Ballard as she stood her fat ass in front of him and pushed him down with one hand.

"And what's that supposed to mean?" she asked stepping to me, before I cold cocked her in the dead center of her nose.

She fell to the ground like a Titan and all the kids laughed as she struggled to get up. I jumped on top of her and punched the dummy until she passed out. She never messed with Jacob or me again.

We were tight from that day forward. Down like two flat tires. We even went to prom together our junior and senior years, because one or the other didn't have a date each year.

We put our friendship over everything. When we graduated high school, we went on to Princeton to complete our college career. To everyone who knew us, it was only right for us to become one. But when Jacob didn't show me that type of attention, I fell hard for my ex-fiancé, Rick, which turned out to be a mistake when he left me at the altar.

Jacob had thrown his life into his family's business. His main interest was keeping his family's legacy alive. I could appreciate that, but there was no place for me in that equation. I tried to work with him and help him with the business, but eventually I got in the way.

Therefore, I was happy when I found Rick; all the way until my wedding day. Jacob watched me fall apart on what was supposed to be my special day, as did three hundred other invited guests when Rick didn't bother to show up. I found out he had another woman and a kid three weeks later when I caught up with him at his job.

I was devastated, but figured Rick was just going along with the wedding because it was my dream to be a beautiful bride. The punk didn't know how to tell me I was his mistress.

Jacob was there through it all. He drove me home from the chapel, speaking life back into my spirit that day, reminding me of the fighter that was within me. Even as the memory of all of those people staring at me, when I stood at the door waiting for my fiancé to show up, made me want to kill myself, he held me close to him and made me promise to be the woman that he knew. He kissed me on the cheek, anticipating my need for affection. That kiss led to a kiss on the other cheek, and then finally my lips. His tongue slipped into my mouth and we melted against one another. The passion behind his kiss was the most intense passion I ever felt.

He glared into my eyes and made me promise to never think about killing myself again. *"Don't you ever leave me,"* he said as he hugged me close. He broke our contact to say, *"I'm sorry for kissing you like that, it's just that..."*

I didn't let him finish his sentence. I pulled him close for another kiss. Before we knew anything, my wedding dress was off my body and on the floor, and Jacob was thrusting his unsheathed penis inside of me. The memory of my fiancé slowly faded away as he made the sweetest love to me.

Our first time was a bitter-sweet memory; one that made me hurt even more when I looked at my cell phone, which had not received one call from him for months, not even to see how I was doing. Not only had he been ignoring my calls, but he also had up and ran off to Georgia behind the first podunk heifer that smiled at him. As one of the richest men in the world, I would have thought he had better sense than that.

I was the kind of classy woman a man of his means was supposed to put on his arm, not Destiny. "What more could he ask for in a potential wife?" I asked myself as I wandered aimlessly around my beautiful home. The amenities Jacob added meant nothing without him around. I plopped down onto the plush sofa, picked up the phone and called him again. My call went to voicemail, once again. This time, he didn't even let it ring but once.

"I tried to give you one last chance, before I took matters into my own hands. Why are you rejecting me?" I yelled, throwing my phone hard against the wall.

Tears sprang from my eyes as I got up from the sofa and rushed into the bedroom.

"This is it! I'm going to end this for once and for all," I said looking at the pistol on my dresser. I put it inside my mouth and willed my finger to squeeze the trigger.

"If we can't be together, I will just end it all," I said, this time pressing as hard as I could against the trigger, but the safety was on. *Damn.*

I sat in the middle of my floor crying, wondering why no one would love me. I picked up my phone and called the Suicide Hotline, which was on speed dial, since I'd sought medical treatment for suicidal thoughts before.

"Hello, this is Stacey from the Suicide Hotline. How may I help you?"

I eased the gun back down and let it fall onto the floor. "I'm about to kill myself, if I don't get need help," I admitted, as I sniveled.

CHAPTER TWENTY-ONE

DESTINY

Interrupted

My eyes opened to find Jacob smiling down on me. "How long have you been awake?" I asked, smiling and running my hand up and down his toned arm.

"Hmm...about an hour."

"You should have got me up."

"You looked like a sleeping angel. I wouldn't dare wake you from your beauty rest."

I moved on the bed, looking around him. "What time is it?"

"It is two o'clock."

"In the morning?"

"Yeah. We still have plenty of time before morning light," he said.

I leaned up and kissed him, wrapping my hand around his neck, and pulling him down so that he was on top of me.

"So I take it you're done sleeping."

"I like the way you think," I said with a smile.

Our kiss deepened, and we held onto the moment. Neither of us made a move to change positions. When we did break our embrace, he slowly moved down my body.

My legs instinctively opened up wider, as he surveyed my glistening mound. He ran his hands down my legs, causing me to shiver. His mouth latched onto my wetness and he plunged his tongue inside. His tongue slid across my clit, causing me to groan. He eased in and out, fucking me fervently with his tongue.

I grabbed onto his head and moved him closer in. I grunted from the slow and sensual movements of his tongue. I moaned, thrusting my hips harder against him, and he went in deeper. His tongue swirled throughout my vagina, picking up any leftover cum from the night of passion we shared.

As he was moving his tongue frantically across my nether lips and up and down my clit, another round of juices flowed out of me. His tongue methodically lapped up every drop.

"Yes!" My head bounced against the bed, as erratic breathing took over my body.

His tongue slowly moved out of its fortress and trailed up to my mouth, where he passionately took over. His hands ran down my sides, while his tongue dipped in and out of my mouth. The fact that we were so absorbed in the moment; it was a wonder that I heard my phone ringing.

"Don't...," he begged, increasing the intensity of his lips on mine.

I ignored it, until it rang again. It was a little after two o'clock in the morning. There was only one person I figured it could be. "I have to," I reluctantly said, pulling away. I reached over the bed and grabbed the phone from my nightstand. I saw his number on the phone. "Hello...Montie?"

"Destiny, I'm sorry for calling so late."

"Are the kids alright?"

"Montana...she has a fever, crying, and nothing I do seems to make her feel better."

I glanced to Jacob, and he was giving me a concerned look. "Have you given her Tylenol?"

"Yes, about two hours ago. All she's doing is yelling for you, though. I would have just brought her home, but Junior is sleeping, and..."

"It's alright. I'm on my way."

I disconnected the call and shot Jacob an apologetic look. Then, I began getting dressed. In the midst of everything, I had forgotten that I didn't have a car. I finished putting my bra on and turned to him.

"I have to go get Montana. She's crying and has a fever. I don't have a car here, so—" I said, when I noticed he was dressing, too.

"I realize that," he replied. "I wouldn't let you go by yourself anyway."

"Thank you."

He shrugged. "No thanks necessary."

****

We rushed to Montie's house. When we got to the door, Jacob remained by my side. I knocked on the door vigorously until he grabbed my hand.

"Give him a chance to get to the door, baby."

"Why is he taking so long?" I was anxious to make sure that Montana got the care she needed.

Montie finally opened the door. He glared at Jacob as if he was not expecting to see him there. I knew he wasn't, but I rushed in with Jacob following me.

"Where is she?" I asked.

"Um…lying down," he mumbled, directing me to the back.

I went into the room and saw her closed eyes.

"I didn't expect you to bring Jacob?" Montie said sarcasm thick in his voice.

"You know, Montie, if I didn't know better I would think that you were up to something," I spat.

He laughed. "Ridiculous."

"Is it?" I asked, looking back to Montana who was sleeping soundly. "Are you sure you didn't just hope you would ruin tonight for me and that's why you called?" I walked over and brushed my hand against her forehead. She was warm, but she didn't have a fever.

"I wouldn't do that," he said defensively.

"I'm not so sure about that."

"I called you, because she wanted you. You took so long that she fell asleep. She can stay since she is sleeping, but I don't want her to wake up again and cry for you."

I shook my head. "You don't have to worry about that. I'm taking her anyway." I leaned down and whispered in her ear, "Montana...baby girl."

"Mommy?" Her eyes fluttered open, and she held her arms out for me to pick her up. She nestled against my neck and drifted back to sleep.

"While I get her ready, go get Junior."

"What? Junior is staying with me. He's fine."

I thought it was crazy to argue the point and just dropped it. I carried Montana out to the living room, where I waited for Montie to rejoin us.

Jacob felt her forehead and a look of concern crossed his face. "She's warm," he whispered.

"Yes, she is," I said touching her forehead again.

"I heard you fussing back there. Is everything okay with you and Montie?"

I nodded, seeing Montie coming down the hallway with Montana's bag.

"Yeah, everything is just fine. You don't have to question her about what she and I talk about. That's between me and Destiny," Montie answered Jacob for me, sounding pissed. "Stay in your own lane."

Jacob calmly walked over to Montie and stood face to face with him. "It seems that you're the one misunderstanding a few things. This..." he turned around and pointed to me with Montana in my arms, "...is my lane. Whatever concerns Destiny, is a major concern of mine and that includes Montie Jr. and Montana."

Montie looked was ready to come back at Jacob, and Jacob didn't look ready to back down. Junior's tiny voice broke into the duel.

"Mommy?" I turned to see Junior standing beside his dad.

"Junior, what are you doing up?" I said as Jacob took a deep breath and walked away from Montie. They were still silently challenging one another.

"What are you doing here, Mommy?" Junior asked, ignoring my question.

"Montana wasn't feeling good, so I'm taking her home. You're going to stay and have a wonderful time with Daddy tomorrow." I was trying to sound cheerful for Montie's sake, but I saw the look on Junior's face as he puckered his lips.

"I want to go home too," he pouted.

"Don't cry, Junior," I said. "It's still your father's weekend time."

"I want to go with you, though," Junior said after a few hard sniffles.

Montie glared at me and I shrugged. It wasn't my fault our kids didn't want to stay with him. I couldn't tell Junior he couldn't go home.

"Go put your shoes on, Junior," I said, and he disappeared back in his room. "I'm sorry, Montie. I couldn't tell him that he couldn't go home. Why don't we just switch weekends? You can have the kids next weekend."

"That won't work. I have to go out of town for work."

"Why doesn't that surprise me? Your work was always most important, so I don't know what to tell you. Montana didn't plan to get sick," I said.

"I know," he grumpily replied and glared at Jacob who had a snarling glare, as well.

Junior came out of the room wearing shoes and carrying his luggage.

"Come on, let's go," Jacob said.

"Bye son," Montie said and hugged Junior.

We left Montie's house with him watching us from the porch. Jacob put the luggage in the trunk and helped to load Junior into the vehicle. I put Montana in her car seat.

"We're going home, sweetie," I said when she briefly opened her eyes. I kissed her forehead and closed her door.

As I got into the passenger seat, I realized Montie had gone inside. He stared out the window with slump shoulders and a look of defeat in his eyes as we drove away.

CHAPTER TWENTY-TWO

DESTINY

Hot and Cold

I walked out of Montana's room, once she was back to sleep, and joined Jacob sitting on the couch in the living room. I sat down beside him, laid my head down his shoulder, and held his hand.

"How's she doing?" he asked.

"She's good. Thanks for standing up for us at Montie's house. I don't know why he acts like that."

"The man lost the best thing that happened to him. I know why he's mad about that, but it's too late. It's my job to love and protect you now. I'm not yielding my responsibilities for one second."

"I love you." I brushed a soft kiss across his lips.

"Mommy?" I pulled from the kiss and turned to find Junior standing in the living room.

"Hey, what are you doing still awake?"

"I can't sleep. Can I sleep with you?" he asked.

"Sure. Go get in my bed and I'll be right there."

Junior ran through the hall and into my bedroom.

"You are a great mom, Destiny," he said.

"You forgive me for cutting our night short?"

"Baby, I wouldn't have had it any other way. Your kids come first, so there is nothing to forgive. Now, if you were the type of woman to put your needs first, that's unforgivable."

"Will I see you tomorrow?" I asked.

"I was thinking about camping out on this couch, if that was alright with you," he patted the couch.

"It's a sweet gesture and I would love to wake up knowing you're in the next room, but that couch won't be very comfortable," I said, taking in his tall stature, which made the furniture look even smaller.

"Oh baby, don't worry about me being comfortable. My comfort comes in knowing that I'm here to protect you all. Now, go take care of Junior and I'll see you tomorrow morning."

I blew a kiss in his direction and smiled all the way to my bedroom. I was going to sleep well.

****

The next morning, I woke up and saw that Junior was still sound asleep. I moved off the bed and padded down the hallway. I peeked in Montana's bedroom. I walked over to her and touched her forehead and was relieved that she wasn't feverish.

I left her room. That's when I smelled bacon. I headed into the kitchen where I stood and watched Jacob as he worked the stove. I couldn't take my eyes off him. I walked over to him and wrapped my arms around his waist, laying my head down on his shoulder.

"Good morning," he said, touching my hand with one of his and flipping the bacon with the other. "Hope you're hungry."

"Hmm..." I moved over to the counter and rested my bottom on the ledge, loving the sight of his domesticated side. "Smells delicious."

He turned off the bacon and put it on a plate. He broke off a piece and put it to my lips.

"Hmm...tastes delicious, too," I said after one bite.

He leaned in and sucked my lips. "You're right, that's pretty delicious."

I smiled and pulled myself from the counter. The waffles had just come up. I helped by getting out a couple plates. "My sleepy heads are still out. They were exhausted," I said.

"There'll be plenty when they wake up," he replied with a wink. I put a plate in front of him and sat down. He joined me. "This gives us a glimpse into what it will be like when we're married, doesn't it?"

"It does," I replied. We never specifically mentioned tying the knot. My marriage to Montie had taken a toll on me. I had prayed for the desire to one day want to marry again. To hear Jacob speak of marriage made me excited about our future. "I want to apologize again, about last night. It was hard to leave your bed and have to deal with Montie."

He shrugged it off. "It just means the next time we're together I'm going to make up for lost time. It turns me on to know that you put your children come first. I love it when a woman has her priorities in order. That's the way it should be."

I munched on a piece of bacon, realizing how blessed I really was. "It means a lot to hear you say that that."

He leaned across the table and we kissed. I nibbled lightly on his syrup covered lower lip and tediously removed the taste from his mouth. I would never tire of kissing Jacob Turner.

"Mommy!" I heard Montana yell from her bedroom. I laughed, pulling away.

"Hot and cold. This is exactly how it would be if we were married. Are you up for it?"

"I'm always up for a challenge. But I know for sure it's going to be more hot than cold, believe that," he said, as I walked away from him and left the kitchen.

I hoped he meant that, because I was going to hold him to it.

CHAPTER TWENTY-THREE

DESTINY

All You Gotta Do Is Say Yes

Over the course of the following week, Jacob and I didn't get to see each other at all. He was busy in Delaware, and my time was occupied with being a mother and PR rep for business, *Genesis,* which was a new business in town. They were an up and coming retail store that I put my touches on to get them known in the market. When the end of the week came around, I tried to think of things the kids, Jacob and I could do that we hadn't already done.

"We could go roller skating," I thought aloud and reached for the phone to call him. Before I picked it up, the phone rang. "You must have read my mind," I answered, assuming that it was Jacob.

"What do you mean, I must have read your mind?" my mother said with an attitude.

"Oh, I thought you were someone else. Hey, Mom...how's it going?"

"It's going good," she answered with a light chuckle. "I would be doing much better if you and my grandchildren had come visit me over the past few months. I've been missing you guys, so I figured I'm going to have to come get my grands, so they can spend the weekend with me."

This was perfect. Junior and Montana could hang with Mom. Jacob and I could pick up where we left off last week. "Mom that's a great idea. You want to keep them this weekend? I've been really busy and that would be helpful," I said.

I didn't want to go into any details about Jacob, so I led her to believe I would be working. I crossed my fingers and hoped she thought it was a great idea, too.

"Bring them over about six o'clock, tonight."

"Sounds great! They are going to love this, Mom."

"Good, see you at six."

I hung up the phone and excitedly called up Jacob. "Hello?"

"Hey, so my mother is going to take the kids this weekend. I'm thinking we can get together and start where we left off last weekend. What do you think?"

"Oh...let me think about that..." my heart fell as he teased me. "I haven't heard anything as good as that this week. That is an amazing idea."

"Good, I will drop them off at six o'clock and head to your place."

"Dinner will be on the table and it'll be just a romantic evening in."

"I love the sound of being curled up in front of the fireplace with a glass of wine and dessert..." I was eager to be there in his arms.

"That and a whole lot extra," he said.

"I can't imagine anything better."

"See you tonight, Destiny. I love you."

"I love you, too."

****

At six o'clock on the nose, I said my goodbyes to my mother and children. I pulled into Jacob's neighborhood at 6:45. I glanced in the mirror to check my makeup. I got out of the car and straightened my red dress. When I reached his door, I knocked and it didn't take long before his arms wrapped lovingly around me and our lips tangled, as if it was our first time. Every time I was with Jacob, it was like our first time. That's how I knew it was meant to be.

"God, I've missed that," I said.

His eyes drank in my dress and a smirk graced his lips. "God, I've missed this," he grabbed a handful of my ass in his hands.

"Behave."

"That I can't promise. Not when the sight of you drives me insane." He hesitantly released me and led me into his dining room. The fragrance was inviting. He held out a chair for me and I took a seat. He then went over and began preparing our meal. "I cooked something you'll like...pork chops and red potatoes."

"I see I'm in for a treat. No man has ever waited on me like this before," I said.

"Remember, I'm not a chef," he teased, putting the plate of food down in front of me. I glanced at the delectable looking food.

"Looks edible to me," I said.

"Judge it when you take a bite."

I cut off a piece from the pork chop and took a bite. "Ugh..." I grimaced.

A look of concern entered his eyes. "I don't usually cook, but I wanted to do something special for you. At least you know I'll do anything for you," he began.

I could not go on with the joke. "It tastes great, actually," I replied, laughing as I took another bite and a drink of the wine. "You did very well, Jacob. I must confess."

"I learned a few things from Greta," he said, referring to his nanny from childhood. He had adoration in his eyes whenever he spoke of her. We talked about how each other's week went, discovering that we both had been waiting for this moment. "This weekend, I'm going to remind you why I'm your man, and I'll repay you for joking about my food," he said, chiming my glass with his.

"Oh..." I scraped empty plate, stuffed. "What do you say, if we just put the dishes in the sink and tomorrow

I help you wash them? Right now, I want to be wrapped up with you, getting punished for my stunning sense of humor."

"You read my mind."

I leaned across the table. "Can you read mine?" I asked, teasing him with a grin.

"You're thinking something naughty. And naughty girls learn the hard way."

I grabbed our dishes and slinked away from the table. I put them in the sink. When I turned around, Jacob greeted me with his hands snaking around my waist. He kissed me, pinning me against the kitchen counter.

"Are you teaching me a lesson?" I softly moaned, pressing my palms into his back.

His arousal grew against me, so I moved past him, grabbing our two glasses and topping them off with wine. I handed a glass to him. He took my hand and guided me to the living room. He leaned down, turned on the electric fireplace, and sat down on the blanket that sat before it. He pulled me down to join him.

"Now, this is what I'm talking about," he said, taking a gulp and putting his glass on a coaster.

We went back into a mesmerizing embrace, where heat and electricity filled our kisses. Our fire toasted the room. He placed me on my back and got on top of me. His tongue swept across mine and my hand dug into his back while we spent time taking it slow. His hands glided to my arms then eased to my back. While I reveled in the romantic moment, he eased the zipper of my dress down, but he didn't go further. He just slipped his hand inside and massaged my back.

I opened his shirt buttons one by one. I didn't remove his shirt, though. I ran my hands over his chest. Our bodies sensually moved against one another, grinding with slow force. My nails trailed down his chest while we intensified the movement of our tongues.

I undid his pants and slid my hand across his erection. He groaned against my mouth, but never broke from our heated kiss. My hand slipped inside his boxers and once again glided over his manhood, but this time without any barrier.

With our eyes locked, I began to remove my dress. Before I slipped it over my shoulders, he spoke.

"Wait..." He stood up and said, "I thought I could, but I can't."

My heart pounded anxiously. I closed my eyes, as I tried to comprehend what was happening. "I don't understand. This isn't the first time we have been together, Jacob. I don't get it."

He placed his hand on mine. "Destiny, look at me."

I opened my eyes. A startled gasp escaped my lips.

He was kneeling before me with a ring in his hand. "I started this day thinking tonight would be a nice romantic evening that ended in some amazing sex.

Then I would propose to you when the time was right, and you would have no doubt in your mind that this was meant to be."

"Jacob..." I whispered. I stared down at the platinum ring with a big ruby in the center surrounded by baguette diamonds.

"Then, you come here wearing that red dress," he smiled showing his beautiful whites, "and we have the nice romantic evening and we are so connected. It just feels...so right. I don't see why I have to wait any longer. This is meant to be and I hope you know that, too. I don't want to go another night without knowing that you are going to be my wife. Destiny, will you marry me?"

Tears streamed down my cheeks. I stared at the ring. "Yes! I will marry you, Jacob." My hands shook as he put the ring on my finger. He pulled me to my feet and took me into a breathtaking embrace, kissing away my fears. He lifted me into his arms and carried me down the hall to his bedroom. He laid me down on the bed and we both wildly removed each other's clothing.

He slid inside of me without warning.

I arched my back to give him better access to what was rightfully his. He dutifully pounded his way inside. He rode harder against me than ever before; the ferocious impact caused me to whimper in pleasurable pain. I lost myself in his violent thrusts.

"Jacob—" I whispered his name into the dimly-lit room.

"Yes baby...," he said, rocking his hips to the sound of my forced breathing.

"Oh Destiny...ahhhh..." he cried, as his cum rapidly forced its way into my womb.

I bucked in a whirlwind of lust. My body shook beneath him, my eyes only opening to look at the spinning ceiling. I fell hard against the bed, searching for a good breath.

"Yes...yes...yes..." I hollered, as I focused on the way his body excited mine. His hands ran up and down my back.

"You feel so good," he moaned, sliding his tongue against mine before trailing down and sucking his way to my shoulder.

"You feel good too," I said on a sigh, breathlessly moaning between each word.

His lips moved to my breasts, latching onto a nipple. He tediously sucked on the left and moved to the right. His teeth caressed each perky nipple, as his tongue slid across the nub.

My sighs turned to ragged sound as if he were trying to regain strength to speak.

He trailed down to my stomach, dipping his tongue inside my navel and swirling it around. He went further south and he licked the juices away from my nether lips. He slid his tongue in and out of my slit, rubbing with torturous movements across my clit.

Aching and throbbing, I wanted to feel his tongue slip in further. It gently moved in, deepening my moans. He flicked hard against my vagina, stroking it with desire.

A deep cry flew out of my lips, and I felt the fluidity of more cum seeping into his mouth. I reached down and grabbed his head, stroking him with pleasure. His tongue maneuvered around my opening, until he was removing himself and ending the pleasure-filled moment.

He rubbed his way up my body, his hands reaching my back and cupping my ass in his palms. He fell down on top of me. His hand reached down and grasped mine. He brought it up to his lips and kissed it.

I stared into his eyes until I drifted off into a dreamless sleep.

CHAPTER TWENTY-FOUR

JACOB

Justine

"Justine!" I woke to beads of sweat running down my face. I sat straight up in bed. My heart was racing. All I could think about was Justine. Something was terribly wrong with her, and I had to get to her, fast.

Destiny sat up in bed, as well. She had a look of concern on her face.

"Jacob, what's wrong?"

"I don't know what it is yet, but something's wrong," I said, as I jumped out of bed. "I have this feeling something is wrong with Justine. The last time I felt like this, she was being rushed to Calvary General after a major overdose."

My mind was racing. I rushed over to my cell phone to see if I had any missed calls. There were none, so I called her.

"Are you calling her?" Destiny asked, and I could see the shock and disappointment on her face as she spoke.

"Yes," I said ending the call. "And she's not answering." I immediately dialed up another number and tapped my feet on the floor as I waited for someone to answer. "Hello, Martha. I'm sorry to call in the middle of the night, but have you or Ron heard from Justine today?"

Destiny stared at me as I spoke. The distress of the turn of events was evident in the way she looked.

"Okay...sure. Have her call me if you do. Thank you!" I hung up the call. "Her parents haven't heard from her either," I told Destiny, as I pulled a T-shirt over my head. "I have to go check on her."

"You're about to go to Miami now?" Destiny asked, as she sat further up in the bed.

"Yeah, I need to go check on her. The last time I felt this way, she had almost killed herself from an overdose."

"Jacob, you haven't talked to her in months. I'm sure she's okay and it was just a bad dream." Destiny said, springing to her feet. She walked over and stood face to face with me.

"No, it's more than that. I know Justine."

"Well," she turned her head sideways and an incredulously daring look entered her glare. "If you know me, you'd come back to bed. You can call and check on her in the morning. Even if something has happened tonight, there is nothing you can do."

She didn't understand why I couldn't leave Justine hanging in a life or death situation. She had shown the ugly part of her character, but still she had been my friend for years.

"You don't understand, Destiny. I can't go to sleep when I can't shake this feeling. You may not get it, but..." My phone rang, interrupting my thought, and I dropped my pants and quickly answered it. "Justine?"

"No, this is not Justine. It's Mallorie, one of the nurses from Calvary General. Is this Jacob Turner?"

"Yes, this is him," I said, shooting Destiny a frantic look.

"Mr. Turner, I have some bad news. Justine Parker has been admitted after being found unconscious at her home today. Her chart has you listed as next of kin, so we need you to come to the hospital as soon as possible so we can make some decisions about her care," the nurse said, and I could hear beeping machines and the busyness of a hospital in the background.

"Is she going to be okay?"

"It's touch and go right now, but she's a fighter. We need you to get here as soon as you can, in case she needs to go on the ventilator."

"I'm on my way," I said, hanging up the phone and going back to getting dressed. "I knew something was wrong," I said as I picked my pants up off the floor.

"Who was that?" Destiny asked, studying my face for answers.

"The hospital in Florida. Justine just got admitted. She overdosed and may need to go on the ventilator. I need to get there ASAP."

"You can't be serious, Jacob. You are running off to Florida because of her?" she said, putting her hands on my pants to stop me from buckling them. "Why don't you just call her parents back and tell them to go."

"Destiny, stop this. I have to go. She is not only my friend, but her parents are my family's friends; and she needs me to be there for her." My head was pounding, as I looked into her eyes and saw the hurt in them. The last thing I wanted to do was hurt Destiny. "You would do this if Montie was in trouble," I said, leveling with her. "And, I wouldn't do anything to stop you."

Her jaw dropped open, and she let go of my pants. "This has nothing to do with Montie! He is the father of my children. She's your crazy ex that uses suicide threats to keep you in line. Besides, you have no real connection to Justine."

"Justine and I have history. We've been friends since kindergarten. You don't know the kind of relationship Justine and I have..." I swallowed the lump in my throat as I remembered my old friend, the one that defended me when I used to be a piss ant.

"You're right. I don't know the relationship you and Justine have," Destiny said somberly.

"I mean the relationship we had," I corrected. "Look, it's not what you're thinking."

Destiny walked over to the closet and stood face to face with me again. "Jacob, just hours ago you made love to me. You asked me to be your wife and to spend the rest of my life with you. Now you're running off to be with your ex-girlfriend," she said, as a tear rolled down her cheek.

I shook my head. "She's an old friend who could be dead by the time I get there. Please understand that this is no more than caring for a friend. It's the right thing to do."

"A friend who has disrespected me on so many levels, more than once."

"She knows not to ever speak that way to you, or about you, ever again. I got that point across to her the last time we talked. And, I'm not going to socialize with her. I'm going to make sure she's physically okay, spend some time with her parents and mine and I'll be returning home." I stepped around her and picked up my suitcase. I placed enough clothes in it for a few days. I slammed the suitcase shut and called Henry. I would call Ron and Martha once I got in my car.

"I need you to come and pick me up right away, and call Tim and tell him to get the jet ready for a trip to Miami pronto."

"Now?" Henry asked, sounding groggy.

"Right now!"

"Okay boss," Henry said, clearing his throat.

I walked over and pulled Destiny close. "Please don't cry, Destiny. You have to know that I love no other woman but you."

"Just go, Jacob," she said pushing me away.

"She needs me, Destiny. We'll talk about this when I get back," I said, torn between my present and my past. I placed a kiss on her forehead and said, "I'm leaving the keys to my car for you to drive home. Lock up when you leave."

Destiny's tears tugged at me as I walked out of the bedroom door and up the hall. I could feel a rip in my heart as I got into the backseat of my car. I couldn't tell what would hurt worse: losing Justine by suicide after having pushed her out of my life, or losing Destiny for trying to be there for a friend.

CHAPTER TWENTY-FIVE

DESTINY

Gon' Learn Today

He cooked me dinner. He asked me to marry him. We made love. Then, a few hours later, he's traveling on his jet to stand beside Justine. It didn't add up. Did he still love Justine? I was tired of her manipulating our relationship. I looked down at my engagement ring and forced those horrible thoughts from my mind. However, the only reason he would wake up out of a dead sleep calling her name was that they had an emotional connection deeper than what he admitted.

"I need you to come and pick me up right away, and call Tim and tell him to get the jet ready for a trip to Miami pronto," he'd said, letting me know that his decision was final. When he hung up the phone, he looked torn, but his next words let me know where his heart was.

"She needs me..." he said before placing a kiss on my forehead. He left our bed of lust, leaving me at a loss for words.

"I need you, too," I whispered as his front door slam shut. More tears threatened to fall as I got up and put my clothes on.

The wonderful smell of his cologne lingering in the air impaled my senses. The look on his face as he made love to me was still fresh on my mind.

Then the fire in his eyes when he said, "*She needs me...*" rushed back. The contents of a person's heart would always shine through. Tonight was that time for Jacob. He and Justine grew up together and she was his best friend before they decided to date. Obviously, they were still fully united. The way he jumped up knowing that something was wrong with her said that they had a deep connection. There was no way in hell or high water I could marry a man that synchronized with another woman.

I brushed my hair back into a ponytail and put on my jacket. Looking around at his mahogany colored room decorated with pictures of American soldiers, I knew it would be my last time in that room. I committed every part of it to memory.

The doorbell rang when I walked out into the hallway. I rushed to the door with a smile on my face. *He came back,* I thought and opened the door without checking to see who it was. I thought Jacob had come to his senses.

"Boo bitch!" Justine said as I stood eye to eye with her chrome-plated pistol. She walked toward me, and I backed up into the house with my hands in the air.

My heart nearly jumped out of my shirt.

"Justine, what are you doing? I thought you were sick."

"Oh, I'm sick; sick of you being with my man, but I have medicine for your ass," Justine said as she pressed the barrel of the gun to my head.

"Ja-cob...is not here. He just got on his jet on the way to Miami to check on you," I said, hoping that would make her back down.

"Don't tell me where my man is! I know where he is. I sent him there. I didn't come for Jacob, Destiny. It's your home-wrecking ass that I'm here to settle up with." Justine's mascara ran wildly down her pale face. She looked as if she hadn't had good sleep in days with disheveled hair and a wild look in her blue eyes.

I continued to back away from her. She drew closer with the gun pointed between my eyes, until I backed into a wall.

"I should kill your black whore ass where you stand. Who do you think you are to try to take my man?" she asked before hitting me on the side of my face with the gun.

"Awwaaw!" Blood gushed from my face and I hollered in pain, while gripping my face with my hand.

"Shut the fuck up before I shut you up. You've been running around here having a ball with Jacob, but this is real life right here. When you take something that belongs to another woman, you have to suffer the consequences. And, there are consequences for taking the one I love."

"I didn't know..." I started to say.

She turned the gun around and hit me with the butt in the center of my face. I fell to the ground, hollering out loudly. I hoped someone would hear me and call the police. Then I remembered Jacob had no neighbors. He'd bought out the entire floor, and the businesses below the condo were closed.

"Wrong answer! I'm not going to let you stand here and act like you didn't know Jacob belonged to me, especially when you saw me at the airport about to kill myself over him. You knew! Bitch, you knew!"

I lay on the ground and watched as she hit her own head with the side of the gun. She took out her cell phone and dialed a series of numbers.

"Move and you will die," she told me while making the calls.

"Hello my darling, Jacob," I heard her say before she kneeled down and popped me with the pistol again.

My head pounded so hard that I couldn't think about moving. The beautiful smiles of my babies flashed before my eyes right as I blacked out.

CHAPTER TWENTY-SIX

JACOB

She Needed Me

My plane ascended into the air. I prayed Justine would make it through her latest suicide attempt, or at least hold on until I got there. I needed to tell her I was sorry for distancing myself from her. I had not taken her calls for the past three months, and the thought of her dying without knowing what she meant to me pierced a piece of my soul. I couldn't believe that, as mentally ill as she'd become, I'd allowed a rift to come between us. I loved Destiny with every part of my manhood, but Justine was there for me when I didn't know how to be there for myself. I should have never left her side knowing she needed me. I owed her my friendship.

"How long will it take to get to Calvary General?" I buzzed the pilot and asked.

"About one and a half hour, sir."

"Cut that down in half and step on it," I said. My cell phone buzzed. I rushed to answer it, when I saw that it was Justine's number. "Hello?"

"Hello my darling, Jacob," Justine said, sounding as calm and regal as ever.

"Justine..." I was relieved to hear her voice, but baffled that she was on the phone. "What are you doing talking on the phone? I just got a call from Calvary General saying that you were hanging on by a thread."

"Oh, I'm far from hanging on by a thread. I can't say the same for Destiny," she said with a wicked laugh. "She's a little under the weather...or should I say under the gun."

"What are you talking about? Are you..." I stopped midsentence, when I recognized Destiny's shrilling scream in the background. I eased forward in my seat. "Justine, who is that hollering?"

Then, I heard it loud and clear. A loud thud, wailing and then silence.

"Oh, that's that cry baby whore of yours. I thought black women were much tougher, but this one is kind of weak Jacob," she said again calm, covering her voice. "She's knocked out now, so she won't be crying for a while, if she ever cries again."

"You better not harm one hair on her head. I swear before everything I know and love that you will pay for this," I said standing up and pacing the aisle.

"Jacob, you've become tough in your adult life, but I'm not scared of you. The hollering is coming from the little nigger that you love so much. You can go ahead and stay in Miami, because you'll have no reason to be

in Atlanta once I put a bullet in her pretty little face."
I could hear Destiny mumbling, obviously pleading for
her life.

"Please don't shoot me," she said weakly.

"Or maybe I'll pop her in her heart so it can stop
beating first. Either way is fine with me, just so long
as she stops breathing."

"You wouldn't do anything like that..." I said,
understanding for the first time the gravity of
Justine's instability. "Justine, don't do this."

"I wouldn't if you had just answered the phone and
talked to me. I wouldn't if you had not walked out on
me. But now, I would and I will. She's as good as
dead..." was the last thing she said before the phone
line went dead.

I rushed to the front of the plane to the cockpit. "Get
me back to Atlanta now!" I told the pilot.

"Right now, boss?"

"Right now!" I screamed.

I tried calling Justine back, but got no answer. The
sad look I left on Destiny's face rushed into my mind.
I would make Justine pay for deceiving me and
hurting Destiny, if it was the last thing I did.

To be continued...

Find out what unfolds in book 2
Available now

Made in the USA
Columbia, SC
01 November 2021